Praise for the Tj J

"Daley's characters come to life ... are filled with a little mystery and a little romance which makes for a murderous adventure."

— Tonya Kappes,
USA Today Bestselling Author of *Fixin' To Die*

"Daley's mysteries offer as much sizzle and pop as fireworks on a hot summer's day."

— Mary Kennedy,
Author of The Dream Club Mysteries

"I'm a huge fan of Kathi's books. I think I've read every one. Without a doubt, she's a gifted cozy mystery author and I eagerly await each new release!"

— Dianne Harman,
Author of the High Desert Cozy Mysteries

"Intriguing, likeable characters, keep-you-guessing mysteries, and settings that literally transport you to Paradise...Daley's stories draw you in and keep you glued until the very last page."

— Tracy Weber,
Agatha-Nominated Author of the Downward Dog Mysteries

"Daley really knows how to write a top-notch cozy."

— *MJB Reviewers*

"Kathi Daley writes a story with a puzzling cold-case mystery while highlighting...the love of home, family, and good friends."

— *Chatting About Cozies*

Puppies
IN
PARADISE

Puppies IN PARADISE

A TJ JENSEN MYSTERY

KATHI DALEY

HENERY PRESS

PUPPIES IN PARADISE
A Tj Jensen Mystery
Part of the Henery Press Mystery Collection

Second Edition | September 2016

Henery Press, LLC
www.henerypress.com

Trade Paperback ISBN-13: 978-1-63511-105-7
Digital epub ISBN-13: 978-1-63511-106-4
Kindle ISBN-13: 978-1-63511-107-1
Hardcover Paperback ISBN-13: 978-1-63511-108-8

Printed in the United States of America

*This book is dedicated to my sister Carrie Zion
for her unwavering love and support.*

ACKNOWLEDGMENTS

They say it takes a village and I have a great one.

I want to thank all my friends who hang out over at my Kathi Daley Books Group page on Facebook. This exceptional group help me not only with promotion but with helpful suggestion and feedback as well.

I want to thank the bloggers who have pretty much adopted me and have helped me to build a fantastic social media presence. There are too many to list but I want to specifically recognize Jenna Czaplewski for participating in all the giveaways.

I want to thank my fellow authors who I run to all the time when I don't know how to do something or how to deal with a situation. I have to say that the cozy mystery family is about as close knit a family as you are likely to find anywhere.

I want to thank Bruce Curran for generously helping me with all my techy questions and Ricky Turner for help with my webpage.

I want to thank my graphic designer Jessica Fisher for all my flashy ads and headers.

I want to thank Randy Ladenheim-Gil for making what I write legible.

I want to thank Art Molinares for welcoming me so enthusiastically to the Henery Press family and a special thank you to Erin George and the entire editing crew who have been so incredibly awesome and fun to work with.

And last but certainly not least, I want to thank my super-husband Ken for allowing me time to write by taking care of everything else (and I mean everything.)

CHAPTER 1

Wednesday, March 11

How do you measure a mental meltdown? Seven thousand, nine hundred, and eighty-two minutes? One hundred thirty-two and two thirds inches? Eighty-three bags of rock salt? Fourteen broken shovels? Five used vacation days?

Tj Jensen loved snow. She really did. She was an avid skier and snowboarder as well as a homegrown mountain girl. It took more than a few flurries to damage her calm, but it had been snowing nonstop for almost six days and she found that she was at the end of her proverbial rope.

Not only were her half-sisters, Ashley (9) and Gracie (6), going stir crazy after being locked up in the house for so long after all of the schools were closed due to the storm, but one of her fellow teachers at Serenity High School, where Tj worked as a physical education teacher and coach, had been in a serious automobile accident that had left her clinging to life in Serenity Community Hospital. Usually with such a serious accident the patient would be airlifted to a larger and better-equipped hospital in the valley, but with the heavy snow and strong wind, moving Stella Blake had been impossible.

Tj wanted to help, but other than taking in Stella's Bernese mountain dog, Kai, and Kai's three adorable but mischievous puppies, there really wasn't much she could do. She knew that Stella was in good hands so Tj shoveled snow and prayed, and then shoveled more snow and prayed some more. Her routine had changed little in the past few days, but with each new shovelful of the white powder, her emotional stability seemed to decrease just a tiny bit.

"I heard we're going to get another eighteen to twenty-four inches before it lets up," Tj's father, Mike Jensen, informed her as they shoveled the walkways at the resort for the sixth time that day.

"Kill me now." Tj groaned as a mound of snow fell from a tree, hitting her squarely on the top of her head. "I feel like we're in the middle of Noah's flood, only with snow instead of rain. I can't help but wonder if it will ever end."

"Maybe we should start working on an ark." Mike chuckled. He'd lived in the Paradise Mountains his entire life and had seen storms much worse than this.

"It'd have to be an ark on ski runners." Tj sighed. She looked at the snow that was piled higher than her five-foot one-inch frame and wondered where they were going to put the snow once they could no longer heave it up onto the wall they had created as they'd maintained the walkways.

"Why don't you take a break?" Mike suggested. "You look exhausted."

Suddenly, Tj's meltdown turned into a guilt fest. Her father was more than twenty years her senior and he wasn't complaining about the back-breaking work that seemed to have taken on a life of its own.

"No, I'm fine." Tj tried to smile. "I'm just worried about Stella."

"Have you heard from Hunter?"

"I talked to him when I went inside to warm up."

"And?" Mike asked.

"He didn't know. Stella is unconscious and in critical condition. It could go either way. I wish I could be there for her."

"I know, sweetheart. But Hunter is a good doctor. She's in good hands."

Hunter Hanson was Tj's friend who might be more than a friend and the chief of staff at Serenity Community Hospital. Although at thirty he might be considered by some to be too young to fill the position, Hunter's grandfather, Jake Hanson, had built the hospital more than sixty years ago, and having a Hanson at the helm had become an expectation. There had never been a doubt in anyone's mind that Hunter would take over as the head of the medical facility once his father retired.

Tj placed her glove-covered hands on the small of her back and leaned into them. She was in good shape, but the endless shoveling was starting to do a number on her muscles. "When exactly is the snow blower supposed to be fixed?"

"I'm not sure. The roads are closed, so we can't go down the mountain to get parts, and the delivery service can't come up the mountain to deliver them. At least we're only partially booked this week. I can't imagine what we'd do if we had to shovel the entire resort."

Maggie's Hideaway, the lakeside resort where Tj lived with her father, grandfather, and two half-sisters, was nestled on the shore of Paradise Lake. It featured a seasonal campground, a twenty-room lodge, and twenty-five individual cabins. The resort hadn't been fully booked when the storm hit, so Mike had moved everyone over to the lodge.

"Have you heard when they might get the roads open?" Tj asked. Not only could they not get parts for the snowblower, but those guests who were at the resort at the time of the closure were stuck there, and everyone with reservations to come up for a ski holiday was unable to do so. Of course the ski resorts were closed as well, so Tj supposed those guests waiting to come up the mountain weren't impacted as much as the ones who wanted to return home.

"So far there's no word on reopening them. I guess it depends on whether the storm lets up a bit." Mike looked up toward the lake, which was completely veiled by the thick wall of snow that seemed to have no end in sight. "The roads around the lake are navigable with a four-wheel drive but all the roads going up and down the mountain are closed indefinitely.

"Do you think they're still going to film the commercial this weekend?" The tourism committee that represented Paradise Lake and the surrounding ski resorts had brought in a crew to film a commercial that would highlight the many wintertime activities the area had to offer. Kyle Donovan, the newest member of the town council, had been asked to show them around, and Tj had agreed to help. The crew had arrived on the same day the storm hit the area, so filming had yet to begin. The committee was lodging the two actors and three camera and technical crew at the inn in town.

"It's hard to say, but the weather report this morning indicated that the storm should pass by Friday. I'm afraid the committee isn't going to be able to keep an actress as popular as Andrea Washburn in the area for much longer. I'm sure she has other commitments. I'm actually kind of surprised she agreed to do the commercial at all," Mike said.

"Kyle said she lived in Serenity when she was younger. She even went to Serenity High School. She was ahead of me in school, so I don't remember her. I asked Kyle about her, and he said she only lived in the area for a short time when she was a teenager. Kyle seems to think that her short residency in the area made quite an impression on her," Tj informed Mike.

"Guess this storm must be making a different kind of impression," Mike speculated.

Tj looked into the sky. The air was so thick with snow she could barely see trees that were just ten yards away. She knew Kyle had worked hard to make the commercial a reality. It would be a shame if it didn't work out. She had to admit, however, that after being snowed in the past week it would be a miracle if Andrea and her costar, Brad Portman, would be able to pull off big smiles as they skied, ice skated, and romped in the snow.

Tj dug her shovel into the snow and continued down the path she was working on. On a positive note, she wouldn't need to go to the gym anytime soon. Trying to keep up with the shoveling when the snow was falling faster than they could remove it had turned into a round-the-clock job for her dad, herself, and the resort staff that had managed to make it out to the property in spite of the road conditions.

Tj paused as she watched her Grandpa Ben make his way

through the snow. She felt bad that he'd been stuck in the house with her sisters and some of their friends. The kids had been bouncing off the walls with suppressed energy, creating an underlying tension that was affecting them all. Tj knew Ben loved the kids, but she also realized he'd rather be shoveling snow with a tablespoon than be cooped up in the house with the kids for six days straight. Yet, unlike Tj, he'd never complained once about the situation that circumstances had thrust upon him.

"What's up?" Tj asked when Ben finally made his way to where she was waiting.

"I think something might have happened to Nolan."

Nolan Rivers was a retired deputy sheriff and one of Ben's best friends. He'd lived in Serenity Nevada since before Tj was born and was considered to be an honorary member of the Jensen family.

"Why do you think that something happened to Nolan?" Tj wondered.

"I was talking to him on the phone about that cold case he's been looking into, and right in the middle of the conversation the phone went dead."

"Maybe he just lost his connection."

"No, it was more than that. We were talking and he said someone was at the door. He set the phone down and I could hear him greet someone, and then there was the sound of a struggle in the background. A few seconds later the line went dead, and he hasn't called me back. It's been an hour and I've tried calling him several times, but it goes straight to voicemail. I'm really worried. I think someone should check on him."

"Maybe we should call the sheriff's office," Tj suggested.

"I did. There was a big pileup on the highway just this side of the road closure. It sounds pretty bad. Everyone is at the scene, trying to save those they can. I know you're busy, but I was hoping you'd be willing to drive me over to Nolan's."

Ben hadn't been cleared to drive since suffering a stroke several years earlier.

"Okay, warm up the truck and I'll tell Dad what we're doing."

The drive into town was slow. Really slow. The snow was falling too fast for the plow drivers to keep the roads clear, and unless you had four-wheel drive with a high clearance you weren't going anywhere. Luckily, the resort owned a workhorse of a truck that had a high-quality drive system and extra high clearance. Still, the falling snow created whiteout conditions, and it was all Tj could do to follow the plow poles that paralleled the road.

Ben sat quietly as Tj drove through the normally busy retail section of Serenity, now all but shut down on account of the storm.

It was odd to see all the dark storefronts in the middle of the day. Serenity was a cute mountain hamlet that had been planned to appeal to the out-of-town visitor. On any other day the mom-and-pop shops that lined the main street paralleling the lake would be lit up like Christmas trees, inviting customers in to warm up with cups of coffee while they shopped for trinkets to remind them of their time on the mountain.

"Looks like Murphy's is open today," Tj said as she

turned off Main Street onto the side street that led to the highway where Nolan's house was located.

"Yup, looks like a full house. Nolan and I spent our share of time warming barstools the last time we were snowed in. I hope it won't be the last time we will be able to do that. I'm really worried about what we're going to find when we get to Nolan's."

"I'm sure it'll be fine," Tj assured the older man, even though she wasn't sure she believed her own statement.

Tj pulled up in front of the two-bedroom house where the retired deputy lived. From the road it looked to be deserted but Tj supposed it was possible that Nolan simply preferred not to turn on the lights in spite of the dark and dreary day.

"The drive hasn't been plowed. I'll go and knock on the door. Why don't you wait here?"

"I'll come with you."

"The snow is pretty deep and I think I'm going to need to use my snowshoes to make it up to the house. I only have the one pair. I'll come right back and let you know what is going on as soon as I find out."

"Okay," Ben agreed with a reluctant tone in his voice. "But be careful. I have a bad feeling."

As Tj began the trek to the front door she was glad she had thought to bring both her snow gear and her snowshoes. If she hadn't she would never have been able to make it from the road to the house without having to wade through the waist deep snow.

"Nolan," Tj called as she knocked on the front door.

When there was no answer she tried the knob and found the door unlocked. She tried to mentally prepare herself for what she might find as she unhooked her snowshoes and left them by the front door. She walked slowly through the small house, calling Nolan's name as she went. The house wasn't big, so it didn't take her long to determine there was no one home. Tj pulled her cell out of her pocket and called Ben.

"There's no one here, and no sign of a struggle," she informed her grandfather. "Maybe he just went out."

"In this weather?"

"Yeah, I guess he wouldn't have gone for a walk, and there were no tracks to indicate that he'd taken his car out of his garage."

"Nolan likes to work out in the shed he converted into an office. If he isn't in the house, there's a good chance he was out there when I was speaking to him."

The shed was located behind the house, so Tj strapped her snowshoes back on and headed out the back door. She was beginning to regret her decision not to bring her dog, Echo, with her. He was always good to have around in a dicey situation, but he'd been playing with Kai's puppies when they'd left and she'd hated to pull him away from the fun he was having. Besides, she'd expected to find Nolan alive and well, with a broken phone or some other logical explanation as to why he hadn't called Ben back after they'd lost their connection.

The shed Ben referred to contained a desk, a sofa, and several file cabinets. Nolan had officially retired as a deputy sheriff quite a few years back, but he liked to poke around in cold cases, so he'd set up the shed as a sort of makeshift squad room. There were maps and whiteboards on all of the walls, as well as bookshelves full of information any good detective might need.

Although there were files on the floor and one file drawer was open, the room was devoid of a human. Tj picked the files up as she looked around for a clue as to what might have happened to Nolan after the phone went dead. She didn't see any blood on the floor, but there was a cup of coffee on the desk, additional open file folders on top of the file cabinets, and smears on the whiteboard where something seemed to have been hastily erased. It looked to Tj as if someone might have broken into the small office.

"He's not out here," Tj reported to Ben after she'd had a moment to look around, "although it looks like he had been out here recently. Any idea where I should look next?"

Tj heard Ben sigh, although he didn't answer right away.

"Do you want to try calling him again?" I suggested.

"I tried while you were walking between the house and the shed," Ben said. "If he was in the shed this morning there should be footprints or at least an indentation in the snow left by his passing. Did you notice anything like that?"

"Yeah. When I came out it was obvious that someone had used snowshoes to get between the house and the shed within the past few hours. The snow along the path is packed down so I'm going to guess that someone accessed the path more than once. I didn't notice any other tracks, so I'm willing to bet Nolan used the same path to get from the shed back to the house. Although," Tj added, realizing that when they'd pulled up to the house there hadn't been any other tracks leading from the street to the house, "if Nolan was already in the house and simply made his way back to the shed there would be only the one set of tracks between the house and the shed. If he struggled with someone, then *the someone* must have entered the property from another direction; there were no tracks from the street to the house when we first arrived. I'm going to look around some more outside. I'll call you back. While I'm doing that, you call Kyle to see if he can run a trace on Nolan's phone with his fancy tracking software."

It was convenient to have a friend like Kyle who was a computer genius able to hack into or track most anything. Before moving to Paradise Lake after his grandfather died and left him his lakefront estate Kyle had been a software developer and a darn good one at that.

Tj strapped her snowshoes back on and headed back out into the storm. Tj really hoped Kyle would find Nolan's phone and that it would lead them to Nolan, alive and well. When Ben had initially asked to come out to check on Nolan Tj had been only mildly concerned, but the longer she looked for the missing man the more concerned she was that he had come to harm.

The shed was situated at the back of Nolan's property. Behind that was national forest. It only took a quick survey of the property to ascertain that someone had indeed snowshoed in through the woods and then accessed the shed from the rear.

Tj followed the tracks, which were mostly covered by this point, for a while before deciding that the snow was falling too heavily for her to risk venturing much farther into the woods. By the time she returned to the shed Ben had spoken to Kyle, who had informed him that Nolan's phone was somewhere on the property.

"I looked all around the shed and I didn't see it," Tj reported. "I'm going to head back to the house and look around some more."

"Be careful," Ben cautioned. "If something did happen to Nolan, whoever harmed him might still be around."

"I'll be careful," Tj promised as she backtracked from the shed toward the house. There were only five rooms in the entire house, and Tj checked each one. The modest-sized living room was furnished with a small sofa, a matching recliner, two end tables, and a large flat-screen television. She looked in the drawers of the end tables, under the cushions of the sofa, and under every piece of furniture before heading to the kitchen and conducting an equally exhaustive search for the missing phone.

When neither the bathroom nor either of the two bedrooms turned up anything, Tj returned to the living room and tried to decide what to do. Kyle was usually spot-on when it came to things like tracking down missing cell phones, so Tj doubted he was wrong in his assertion that the phone was on the property. She'd checked the shed and the house, which left only the garage. There'd been no evidence to indicate that Nolan had removed the car from the garage since the snow had begun to fall, so she hadn't previously thought to look there.

The garage was dark and the bulb from the overhead light was burned out, so Tj accessed the flashlight on her cell phone and searched the building as carefully as she could. There were boxes and discarded furniture stacked along each wall, but she could see the car was parked in its usual spot in the center of the clutter. She had no idea where to start given the sheer number of items to look through.

Although there didn't appear to be anything out of place, the garage smelled like exhaust, and Tj noticed that someone had opened a small window that was hidden behind a tall tool cabinet. She was about to return to her truck when a little voice in her head prompted her to look inside the car, which didn't appear to have been moved recently based on the fact that Nolan had parked his snowblower behind it. Tj walked over to the car and peered inside. At first glance she didn't see anything in the dim light and there was nothing on the front seat, but a quick glance toward the backseat revealed the lifeless body of Nolan Rivers, slumped over in an odd position.

CHAPTER 2

After Tj spoke to local deputies Tim Mathews and Roy Fisher, telling them everything she knew, she decided to stop by the hospital to check in on Stella. It had been several days since the accident, and her condition hadn't really changed, but as long as she was already in town, it wouldn't hurt to speak to Hunter personally about her prognosis. Ben had been understandably upset by the situation with Nolan so Tj had dropped him off at Murphy's for a cold one while she visited her friend.

"She looks so frail," Tj whispered to Hunter as they stood by Stella's bed. Stella had swerved to avoid contact with an oncoming vehicle which had slid on the ice and veered into her lane. She avoided the collision only to plummet down the steep embankment to her right causing her car to roll three times before hitting a tree. Driving on narrow and winding mountain roads was always somewhat risky but especially dangerous during a storm.

"Her injuries are very serious," Hunter confirmed. "She has several broken bones that will mend, and cuts and bruises that will heal, but the head injury isn't looking good.

I've done everything I can, but I honestly can't say whether she'll wake up or not. I've called to consult with several specialists who've assured me that we're doing everything we can to help her fight her way back, but at this point it's up to her."

Hunter squeezed Tj's shoulder as she lay her head against his arm.

"When do you think you'll know?" Tj asked.

"It's hard to tell. She has swelling in her brain that could be causing her state of unconsciousness. We hope that once the swelling subsides she'll wake up on her own. She's breathing on her own, which is a good sign. Her vitals are holding steady and she isn't in any immediate danger. All we can do at this point is monitor the situation and wait. How are you holding up?"

"Honestly? Not that great. I have Kai and the puppies at the resort, but Kai seems to know that something is up and has taken to pacing and panting when she isn't caring for her babies. I feel bad for her, so on top of stressing over Stella's recovery I find myself stressing over Kai's anxiety and her disinclination to eat, especially since I know that a nursing mom needs lots of nutrients. And then there are the puppies. Don't get me wrong, they're super cute, but they're at that destroy-the-house-and-pee-on-every-flooring-surface phase. It's too cold to keep them in the barn, and I can't keep them crated all day, so I set up a room with a plastic liner and tons of piddle papers and am letting them out onto the covered patio area as much as possible. The rest of the time I'm chasing them around with spot treatment. Then, to top it all off, the snowblower at the resort is broken and we can't get parts up the hill due to the road closure, so Dad and I have been trying to keep the place dug out by hand while Grandpa watches the girls, who, by the way, are bouncing off the walls with unspent energy. Of course now poor Grandpa is so devastated about what happened to Nolan that I'm not sure if he'll be able to continue to handle two hyper grade-schoolers with the sniffles who absolutely cannot go outside. Oh, and don't even get me started on..." Tj stopped speaking and laughed. "I guess you weren't really asking about all of that, were you?"

"Not really, but it's fine. You obviously needed to vent. It's been a tough week for everyone. I wish I could help, but to be honest, I've been swamped."

Tj wrapped her arm around Hunter's waist and let his warmth calm her. "I know. I'm sorry for the rant. I guess things have just been building up, and now that Nolan's dead, I just don't know how we're going to get through this. Who would do such a thing?"

"What exactly do Tim and Roy think happened?" Hunter asked.

"Based on the evidence they could find, it looked like someone knocked him out and then drug him back to the house where they deposited him in his car. They then turned on the motor and asphyxiated him."

"Was the car still running when you arrived?" Hunter asked.

"No, but I could smell the exhaust. It appears that whoever killed Nolan used a hose to pump the exhaust directly into the car for maximum effect. They didn't find the hose on the property, but based on the timeline it seemed clear that the exhaust was channeled into the vehicle. Before he left, the killer turned off the car and opened a window to air out the garage, but there was still the scent of exhaust in the air."

"Based on the fact that the murder was carried out in such a way as to be painless to Nolan, it seems like the killer knew him."

Tj frowned. "As odd as it sounds, you could be right. Grandpa was on the phone with Nolan when someone came to the door. He heard Nolan greet the person and then heard a struggle, so we're assuming Nolan invited his killer in."

"The guy must have acted quickly to accomplish all of that before you got there," Hunter hypothesized.

"Yeah. We think it was about two hours between the time Grandpa was speaking to Nolan and the time we found his body. Doc is doing an autopsy as we speak. Hopefully we'll know more when he's done."

Doc, a.k.a. Stan Griffin, was a retired coroner who helped out the Paradise County Sheriff on occasion.

Tj looked at her watch. "I really should go pick up Grandpa. I left him at Murphy's. If I leave him there too long, I may have another problem to deal with."

"Barring any new emergencies, I should get off in a couple of hours. Do you want me to come over?"

Tj hesitated. "You look awfully tired."

"So do you. But if you want to talk..."

"Kyle is coming over, and I'm sure Doc will come by when he's done here, but yeah, I'd love for you to come by if you're up to it."

Three hours later, Ben, Mike, Doc, Kyle, and Tj were all sitting around the kitchen table at the resort drinking coffee.

Hunter had called to say there'd been another major accident, so he was going to be stuck at the hospital for most of the night. Kyle and Tj had taken Echo, Kai, and Kyle's dog, Trooper, out for a quick run while Mike got the girls tucked into bed, and Ben sat with Doc as they memorialized their friend and questioned a universe where something like this could happen.

Sure, Nolan was an ex-deputy, and as a deputy he'd made some enemies, but he'd been retired a long time and most folks seemed to like and respect him. Ben acknowledged that Nolan had been poking around in some cold cases to pass the time, which led to a discussion centered on the theory that he had stumbled across something that someone didn't want to be found.

"Do you know what he was working on?" Tj asked Ben as he stirred his coffee in a robotic manner.

"He had two or three cases he was looking into. I'm not sure what all he was pursuing at the moment, but we were talking about the young couple who were killed in that fire fifteen or so years ago when he…" Ben stopped talking. It was obvious he was choked up and couldn't continue.

Tj tried to remember what he was referring to. She'd only been a teenager at the time, but she seemed to remember that a pair of newlyweds had been tied up and then died in a fire that had been set intentionally.

"If I remember correctly they arrested a man who they were certain was guilty of the crime. He had a known beef with the couple and a history of arson. It seemed like it was going to be an open-and-shut case, but they ended up releasing him when another fire with the same signature occurred while he was in lockup," Ben recalled.

"Signature?" Kyle asked.

"I'm not an expert on fire investigation but I know from talking to the guys down at the firehouse that arsonists tend to follow a similar pattern with each fire they set. They use the same accelerant and same ignition device causing a similar burn pattern. I guess the details are so specific as to leave a signature of sorts. Nolan was sure the guy they'd arrested was guilty in spite of the fact that the evidence seemed to indicate otherwise. He felt the man was released too quickly, but he didn't have a lot of control over the situation. According to Nolan, they never did make an arrest in either fire."

"Did he have any theories as to who might have killed the couple?" Kyle asked.

"I don't know. He said he had some ideas he was going to follow up on, but he wouldn't say exactly what those ideas were."

"You know," Mike contributed, "I seem to remember reading a newspaper article that claimed the case had been handled sloppily from the start. I can't remember the details, but it may very well be that Nolan wasn't all that far off in his assumption that things weren't as clear as they made them out to be."

Tj got up to refill coffee cups as the conversation continued. A quick glance out the window confirmed that it was still snowing heavily. The roads would be slicker than they'd been during the day, and visibility was close to zero. The cabins were empty because her dad had moved everyone over to the inn and therefore available for overnight guests. Tj decided she would encourage Doc and Kyle to stay the night rather than risk another tragedy.

"What else was he working on?" Kyle asked as Tj returned to the group.

"That mutilated body that was found buried with another body awhile back," Ben answered.

"I remember that," Tj shared as she stirred sugar into her coffee. "The family of a woman who had been dead for a number of years had her body exhumed after her granddaughter confessed that when her grandmother was buried she had slipped a very expensive necklace in the coffin with her. The family believed that the necklace had simply been misplaced, but when the family fell on hard times and almost lost their home, the granddaughter came clean. When they opened the coffin they found a second body buried with the first that as far as I know was never identified."

"Wow, that would be a shock for the cemetery worker hired to dig up the grave," Kyle commented.

"Yeah, it was pretty bad. It seemed the body had been dismembered. All the fingers and teeth were missing. Someone didn't want the body to be identified. All they really know for certain is that the victim was male."

"I suppose if Nolan figured out who the second body belonged to that might get him killed," Doc speculated.

"Did Nolan tell you anything specific about either cold case?" Tj asked Ben.

"Not really. You know Nolan. He was always intentionally vague when he was working a case. I do know he pulled a bunch of old arrest files. He seemed to think there was more going on than met the eye."

"We need to go back to get his files," Tj said. "It's the only way we're ever going to find out what bit of information it was that got Nolan killed."

"I'm sure the sheriff's office has secured the area," Mike asserted. "Besides, it's pitch black out and the snow is coming down as heavily as ever."

"Mike is right," Doc agreed. "Besides, you indicated that the files could've been disturbed, so chances are the killer took whatever files they wanted buried before you arrived."

"It seems like we should still *try* to find out what Nolan was on to," Tj insisted.

"Maybe he kept notes on his computer," Kyle said. "I can go over there tomorrow to see if I can find it. If I can get hold of the computer, I can recover whatever might be on the hard drive."

"As long as you're there you should get the files," Doc added. "I'd come with you, but I'm due at the hospital. They're asking everyone to pitch in until the storm is over."

"We're bound to have a long day tomorrow. Maybe we should all get some sleep and pick this up in the morning," Mike suggested.

"I think it would be best if Doc and Kyle stayed over. You can camp out in one of the empty cabins," Tj said.

Both men agreed to the plan, even though it required digging their way into the cabins, which hadn't been shoveled out yet.

After everyone was settled Tj dragged herself up the stairs. She knew it would only be a few hours before she'd have to get up and continue with her shoveling marathon, but in the meantime all she wanted to do was climb into her big bed with the flannel sheets and down comforter and rest her tired, achy body.

Her cat, Cuervo, followed her up the stairs the moment he realized it was bedtime, but Echo was nowhere to be found, which was odd because he rarely left Tj's side. She knew he was fascinated with the puppies, so she went into the spare room, where they'd laid down the plastic flooring, old rugs, and newspaper for the little family, only to find the room empty. Completely empty. Apparently, all five dogs were missing.

Tj suspected that Gracie was somehow involved in the case of the missing dogs, so she quietly made her way down the hall and peeked into her door. Sure enough, both adult dogs were sleeping on the rug next to Gracie's bed and all three puppies were sleeping on top of her covers. Tj had to smile. Even Gracie's cat, Crissy, had decided to welcome the furry visitors. Tj hated to wake them, but she realized the puppies would most likely wake up at some point during the night and she didn't want them falling off the bed. She should return them to the pen they'd created for them, but Kai seemed more content here than she'd been since she'd been at the resort, so instead of moving them all into the adjoining room she decided to simply move them to the floor, where they could curl up with Mama and Uncle Echo. A few additional puppy piddles weren't going to make that much difference at this point anyway. The carpet was going to need to be professionally cleaned, or possibly even replaced, by the time Kai and her babies went home.

"Tj," Gracie said tiredly as her sister picked up the first puppy.

"Go back to sleep, sweetheart. I'm just going to put the puppies on the floor."

"But they want to sleep with me."

"I know. But they're so little that they could get hurt if they fell off your big bed. It's better for them on the floor. It was nice of you to let them sleep in here with you."

"Kai is sad. She misses her mommy."

"Yeah, I know she does."

"Is she going to be better soon?" Gracie wondered.

Tj hesitated. Ever since losing her own mother in an accident, Gracie had been super sensitive to other people or animals who didn't have mothers. Even though Stella wasn't technically Kai's mother, Tj knew Gracie interpreted the relationship in exactly that way.

"I'm not sure when Stella is going to be able to get out of the hospital, but Kai and the puppies have us to take care of them in the meantime, so I'm sure they'll be fine."

"Can we put my bed on the floor?"

Tj hesitated.

"Just for tonight, so I can help Kai take care of her babies the way you took care of me and Ashley when Mom died."

"Sure," Tj decided. "I don't suppose it would hurt to put your mattress on the floor for one night." Even as Tj said the words, she knew Gracie's mattress would remain on the floor for the duration of the puppies' stay.

CHAPTER 3

Thursday, March 12

By the next morning it looked like the storm might be tapering off. It was still snowing, but the blizzard had gentled into a softly falling curtain of small flakes that floated in the now still air. Tj checked in with her grandfather, who was making breakfast for the kids, before bundling up to help her dad shovel the snow that had fallen overnight.

Doc had headed into town before sunup to shower and change before heading over to the hospital for his shift, but Kyle volunteered to help with the shoveling, which moved things along much faster. Although the storm was beginning to pass, the town had postponed the return to school to Monday to give everyone a chance to dig out. Tj found she was happy that she had a few additional days before going back to work; it would give her time to poke around in Nolan's death a bit before returning to the demands of the statewide downhill race the high school team she coached was participating in later in the month.

"Something smells good," Tj said appreciatively when she came in from shoveling.

"I have hot coffee, pancakes, bacon, and scrambled eggs warming for you." Ben handed both Kyle and Tj cups of the steaming brew. "Is your dad far behind?"

"He should only be a few more minutes. He wanted to check with the front desk before he headed in. Are the kids upstairs?"

"They're watching cartoons in the den." Ben slid plates full of food in front of Tj and Kyle, who had sat down at the bar that separated the cooking from the eating area.

"How are you doing this morning?" Tj asked.

"Been better," Ben admitted.

"I'm sorry, Grandpa." Tj's heart bled for the man who had lost one of his best friends.

"You still planning to look for Nolan's computer?" Ben asked Kyle.

"As soon as I finish this delicious breakfast you made I'm going to call Roy and ask him about gaining access," Kyle confirmed. "Hopefully the killer didn't have the presence of mind to take it."

"Nolan kept his laptop in the bottom of his bureau, under his t-shirts. He once told me that people never think to look under the t-shirts, although they usually look in the underwear drawer."

"Thanks. It will make my job quicker if I know where to look," Kyle said.

"I hope we can find whoever did this. Nolan deserves to have his killer brought to justice," Ben proclaimed.

"We'll figure out who did this," Tj promised.

"I want to help. I need to help," Ben insisted. "Nolan has

been an important part of this family and this community for as long as I've lived here. He has been there for all of us in the past and I think we need to pull together to make sure the person responsible for his untimely death is brought to justice."

Tj's heart broke when she noticed a tear in her grandpa's eye. She looked at Kyle. "I guess we could all meet back here tonight to discuss a strategy."

Kyle shrugged. "I'm in."

"I'll make spaghetti," Ben offered. "Maybe Doc will be freed up to come out as well."

Tj called Jenna that morning to inform her of Nolan's death. Jenna was her best friend, and she usually would have called her right away, but everything had happened so fast that it had completely slipped her mind. Jenna planned to spend the day at the Antiquery, the café/antique store she owned with her mother Helen, preparing for its reopening the following day, so Tj promised to come by when she'd finished her shoveling to fill her in on everything that had happened so far.

Kyle finished breakfast and headed into town to retrieve Nolan's computer and anything else he could find that seemed relevant to the case. By the time Tj followed him into town herself, the snow had stopped, at least temporarily, and the area plow teams were out in full force.

"I see you survived the blizzard," Tj greeted Jenna as she pulled off her hat and mittens. She tucked them in the pockets of her red ski jacket before hanging it on a peg near the back door of the restaurant.

"Just barely. Having the kids cooped up in the house for a week was its own kind of adventure."

"Tell me about it, although at least I had Grandpa to help out. Is Kari still sick?" Tj asked about Jenna's younger daughter.

"She's feeling better, but now I'm afraid Kristi is coming down with her flu. I'm hoping it will pass before school starts back up on Monday."

"Is Dennis on shift?" Tj asked about Jenna's firefighter husband.

"With all the accidents, he's worked every day since the storm blew in. The overtime will be nice—it might even allow us to go on the trip we've been talking about taking—but I know he's exhausted."

"Trip?"

Jenna scooped the measuring cup into the bag of flour she had set on the counter and dumped it into the bowl of bread dough she was mixing up. "We're hoping to get away for a week or two when Dennis takes his vacation time. Of course, I still need to work out after-school care for the girls, but I'm sure Mom will watch them when she isn't working."

"I can help out," Tj offered. "I'm sure Grandpa will help as well."

"Thanks." Jenna adjusted the net over her long blond hair. "I really appreciate that."

"I'm happy to have the opportunity to repay one of the seven million favors I owe you. Where are you thinking of going?"

"We really wanted to do something tropical like Hawaii, but we didn't think we could afford it. Now, with all the overtime, maybe."

"Hawaii sounds wonderful. In fact, anywhere that doesn't have ten feet of snow sounds wonderful."

"I thought you liked snow," Jenna reminded her.

"I do, but I think I've had my share of shoveling for the year. Though I can't wait until the ski resorts reopen so I can get at all that beautiful powder."

Jenna turned the dough onto the large counter she was working on and began to knead it. "By the way, I checked the girls' room and didn't find Gracie's jacket or her red mittens. Did you recheck the lost and found at school?"

"They aren't there. So far she's lost two fairly expensive jackets, four sets of mittens, the new scarf she got for Christmas, and two knitted hats this year. I'm about at the end of my rope."

"Have you tried talking to her about a plan to keep track of her things?"

"I have. I even tried punishing her, but then she spilled a couple of those huge crocodile tears she's famous for and I caved in and just gave her another warning."

"You know you can't let her manipulate you like that."

Tj sighed. "Yeah, I know. I guess I'll just buy her another jacket. She'll need one for school on Monday and it isn't like she can go without."

"I think Grainger's has jackets on sale. Be sure to put her name in it, and you might want to talk to her ahead of time about the consequence if she loses this one."

"That's a good idea. I need to sit down and talk to her about the puppies anyway."

"Puppies?"

"Kai's puppies. I'm dogsitting while Stella's in the hospital and Gracie has latched on to those puppies like they're hers. She talks about them as if they're going to become a permanent part of our household. I've tried to explain to her that they all have new homes to go to when they're old enough, but when I went by her room this morning she was talking to them about the fun they're going to have together this summer."

"Has she named them?" Jenna asked as she placed the dough under the heat lamp to rise.

"Afraid so. And they slept in her room last night. I was in a hurry this morning, but when I get home I'm going to have to make her understand that the puppies aren't at the resort to stay."

"How's Stella doing?" Jenna asked as she began gathering ingredients for her next project.

"The same. Stable, but still unconscious. Now that the storm has let up they're talking about moving her down the mountain, but Hunter thinks it's too risky at this point. He seems to think she's starting to come out of it, so he's going to continue to monitor the situation for another day or two."

"Poor thing. It really is so tragic."

"I stopped by to see her yesterday and she didn't even look like the same person. I just hope she wakes up today. Hunter said that otherwise she seems to be healing nicely."

Jenna turned on the mixer, pausing their conversation temporarily. Tj always loved sitting in Jenna's kitchen while she baked. The smell was heavenly, and she usually could manage to snag a sample of whatever delicious offering her friend was baking at the moment. Today, the smell of cinnamon and vanilla filled the air. It was warm in the kitchen, but a glance out the window revealed that it was snowing lightly once again.

"Any news on Nolan's murder?" Jenna asked once she'd turned off the mixer.

"No, not really. Kyle and I are going to follow up on a few things, but there really wasn't any evidence at the scene to suggest who might have interrupted the conversation grandpa was having with Nolan." Tj took a sip of her coffee. "The worst part about this whole thing, other than the fact that a wonderful man who meant the world to a lot of people is dead, is the fact that it appears as if Nolan knew his killer. Grandpa clearly heard Nolan invite someone to come inside before the struggle occurred, which we assume ended with Nolan's death."

"I can't imagine anyone who knew Nolan would want to kill him. He was such an easy going guy. He really didn't seem to have any enemies."

"Grandpa thinks that the motive for his murder has to do with one of the cold cases he was working on and I tend to agree."

"Do you know what he was looking into?" Jenna asked.

"Grandpa said he was looking into the fire that killed that young couple when we were teenagers along with the extra body that was found in that old woman's coffin when she was exhumed to retrieve the bracelet her granddaughter had slipped inside prior to her burial. He seemed to think there might have been a few other cases that he was looking into but those were the two that came to mind."

Jenna stopped what she was doing and leaned back against the counter behind her. She crossed her arms over her chest. "I just can't believe Nolan is gone. It still seems so surreal. I don't have the sleuthing gene the way you seem to, but if there is anything at all I can do to help just ask."

"Thanks. I will. One way or another we are going to get the person who did this and bring them to justice."

After Tj left the Antiquery she headed to the hardware store to pick up the supplies she'd promised her dad she would purchase while she was in town.

The shops along the main drag were slowly beginning to reopen now that the storm had passed, so she figured she'd stop off at the post office to see if Hazel had been able to make it in as well. The lights were on and the open sign was prominently displayed. She should have known it would take more than a little snow to keep the seventy-five-year-old postmistress away for long.

"Morning, Hazel," Tj called as she stomped the snow from her boots.

"I'm afraid we haven't had a mail delivery from the valley since the road closed," Hazel informed her. "I'm hoping the truck can get up the mountain today to deliver the backlog. Still, it'll take me a day or so to get everything sorted, so you might want to check back tomorrow. Were you expecting something important?"

"No. I was in town to pick up some supplies for Dad and saw your lights on, so I thought I'd stop by to say hi."

"Folks have been dropping by all morning to see if I have any news about Nolan," Hazel said.

"And do you?" Tj asked. "Have any news?"

"Not really. There's a lot of speculation, but you know I don't like to gossip."

Tj suppressed a smile. Everyone knew Hazel loved to gossip.

"So what does everyone think happened?" Tj wondered. She doubted the local gossip line would yield any actual leads, but it never hurt to ask.

"No one claims to have seen Nolan since the storm hit, but there are a few folks who saw him in town the day before it blew in. Based on the stops he made, I'd say he was looking into something. Probably one of his cold cases."

"Yeah, Grandpa said he was working on a couple of those old cases he likes to tinker with. Do you happen to know where he went on the day before the storm?"

"He had lunch at Murphy's, but it seemed like he was alone because a couple of folks mentioned he was sitting at the bar. Harley said he ran into him at the shooting range earlier that morning."

Tj knew that, as an ex-cop, Nolan enjoyed shooting a few rounds every now and then. He'd once told her that he liked to prove to himself that he still had what it took to shoot with accuracy in spite of his advancing age. It also wasn't odd that Nolan would stop off to have lunch at Murphy's. Murphy and Nolan were friends, and everyone knew Nolan often ate at the bar.

"Spending time at the shooting range and eating lunch at Murphy's seems like routine behavior," Tj pointed out. "Why do people think he was investigating one of his cases that day?"

"I guess it was the fact that he was seen at the feed store, yet he didn't have any pets, and Harriet saw him talking to Brandon Halliwell when she was in Rita's, buying flowers for a sick friend. Harriet couldn't hear what they were saying, but she said it seemed like they were arguing, so she asked Brandon about it after Nolan left. Brandon told her Nolan was thinking about ordering a new gun for his collection."

Tj frowned. "Let me get this straight. Nolan went to the shooting range, which he often does, and then he had lunch at Murphy's, which he also often does. After lunch he stopped off to talk to Dover at the feed store, which isn't really all that odd considering the two men were friends, and then he went to Guns and Roses to talk to Brandon about a new gun. All of these activities seem routine for Nolan. Why do folks think it was odd?"

"Because he had his little notebook out and was making notes at each stop," Hazel explained.

"Yeah, well, I guess that might seem odd."

Tj realized she needed to find that notebook. If Nolan was researching a case maybe the notes he took that day would lead them to the killer.

Tj called Kyle to ask him to look for the notebook while he was at Nolan's. Kyle informed her that he had already been to Nolan's and had retrieved the computer, as well as all the files he could find, but he hadn't seen a notebook. He promised to go back to specifically look for a notebook on his way out to the resort. Kyle had already been looking over Nolan's hard drive, so he might have some news when he got there.

By the time Kyle pulled into the drive in front of the house, Tj had worked herself into a state of nervous anticipation. She hoped Nolan had left behind clues that would help them identify his killer. He'd been a cop for a lot of years, and as a cop he'd learned to chronicle his movements.

"Something smells good in here," Kyle commented as he stomped the snow from his boots.

"Spaghetti and garlic bread," Ben replied.

"Sounds fantastic."

"So, do you have news?" Tj jumped right in.

"I do have news." Kyle nodded. "Sort of. What I really have is a new set of questions."

"Questions are a place to start," Tj said.

"Doc should be here in a few minutes, and Mike is going to join us as soon as he finishes up in the lodge," Ben told the pair.

Kyle took off his jacket and hung it on the peg next to Tj's. He laid a file folder on the table in front of where Tj was sitting before pouring himself a cup of coffee.

"I spoke to Roy earlier," Kyle informed Tj and Ben. "He admitted they're coming up short on suspects. Whoever killed Nolan parked on that old service road that runs behind his property and then snowshoed in."

Tj frowned. "There's no way that old road would be plowed."

"It wasn't. The intruder came on snowmobile. The snow was falling hard enough that the snowmobile tracks were partially covered but the ruts in the snow left by the heavy machine were still discernable. Roy said they lead back to the main highway and then disappear. Roy figures the killer must have had a truck parked on the highway that transported the snowmobile to and from the entry point. That's actually unfortunate because snowmobile tracks would have been easier to follow than tire tracks on a road that has since been plowed."

"And then, once the killer got close enough to the house,

where the noise from the snowmobile would have been heard, he switched to snowshoes," Tj concluded.

"That's how it looks," Kyle agreed.

"I guess that doesn't give us much information, but it does tell us that the killer has access to a snowmobile and snowshoes and is familiar with the area," Ben commented. "Did the sheriff's office find anything else?"

"They think the killer weighed two hundred pounds or more, based on the depth of the snowshoe tracks. It was snowing heavily and the tracks were pretty much covered by the time they checked them out, but they were able to estimate based on the rate of snowfall and the deepest impression of the prints that they were made by someone heavy."

"That makes sense," Tj said. "Nolan was getting on in years, but he was in pretty good shape, and he knew self-defense moves. I doubt a small person could take him down."

She opened the file. The top piece of paper looked to be a copy of a police report. It was dated fifteen years earlier and related to the fire that had killed the young couple and resulted in the temporary confinement of Clay Warner.

"Nolan had a copy of the arrest file for the fire," Tj noted. "So what? We already knew Warner was arrested and later released."

"What I found interesting in the file is that the name of the arresting officer has been blacked out. It's a copy of the original, and Nolan may have blacked out the name himself, but in the event that the original also had the name blacked out, I would find that very interesting indeed."

"Why would anyone black out the name of the arresting officer? That must be public record," Tj stated.

"You would think so, but I did several searches and couldn't find any similar record where the arresting officer's name was mentioned."

"Can you get the original file?" Tj asked.

"I may be able to dig it up, but I decided that asking Roy to get it would be easier. I stopped by the sheriff's office on the way over. Roy said he'd look into getting the original police report sent from the county offices. I also found a copy of a note from the district attorney stating that, due to the circumstances, he wouldn't be able to prosecute the case as it stood," Kyle said.

"What circumstances?" Ben asked.

"They must be referring to that second fire with the same signature while Warner was in jail," Tj hypothesized.

"That's what I thought as well at first, but if you look at the date of the second fire and then at the date of the note from the district attorney, you'll find that the note came before the second fire," Kyle responded.

"So there were problems with the arrest prior to the second fire," Tj concluded. "Any idea what those were?"

Kyle shook his head. "I haven't found anything so far, but I plan to keep looking."

Ben slipped his hands into oven mitts before taking the bread out of the oven. "What I don't get is, how can any of this relate to Nolan's death? The records you found are from a long time ago."

"We don't know for certain that the cold cases Nolan was working on have anything to do with his death," Kyle said. "We just needed a place to start."

"Did Roy happen to mention whether they had any leads while you were there?" Tj asked Kyle.

"He didn't say, but he didn't seem overly surprised when I asked him to pull the original arrest record for Clay Warner. If I had to guess, he's thinking along the same lines we are."

"Looks like Doc just pulled up, and I can see Mike heading this way," Ben interrupted the conversation. "Let's go ahead and eat and then pick this up later."

Despite the fact that Ben was in deep grieving, he'd managed to put together a delicious meal. The conversation around the dinner table centered mostly on the puppies and how cute they were, as well as their plans for the next few days.

Tj took a moment to enjoy the warmth on her back from the brick fireplace that heated the kitchen and dining area. After the long and difficult week, it was nice to share a meal with family and friends. Ashley had talked Kyle into taking her and a couple of her friends to a movie, and Tj smiled at the artful way she'd manipulated him into doing exactly what she wanted him to do. Kyle was a huge pushover who could never seem to say no, and the girls took advantage of his good nature more often than they should.

Of course Tj realized it would give him a reason to spend some quality time with Annabeth, the thirteen-year-old girl for whom he had accepted guardianship when her father had been arrested the previous summer. Annabeth lived in town with his mother rather than at Kyle's lakeside estate, but he tried to spend as much time with her as he could. By the time Ashley had finished hoodwinking him, he had agreed to take eight girls to the newest Disney release.

After dinner Tj, Kyle, Ben, Mike, and Doc sat around the dining table, trying to work out a strategy, while Ashley and Gracie watched a video. Tj felt bad about the girls being relegated to the den as often as they had this week, but sometimes settling them in front of the electronic babysitter was the most efficient way for Tj to juggle the many different things she spent a good part of her life managing.

Everyone poured themselves the beverage of their choice and Kyle filled Mike and Doc in on the conversation he'd had with Tj and Ben before dinner.

"So it looks like Clay Warner might have been off the hook even before the second fire?" Mike confirmed after everyone had been brought up to speed.

"Based on the note I found from the district attorney, I would say that's a correct assumption." Kyle nodded.

"Maybe we should interview the DA to see what he meant in his note," Tj suggested.

"Can't," Ben informed her. "He died a good five years ago."

Tj sighed. Of course he did. A cryptic note from a dead man probably wasn't going to provide them with very much information unless there was other correspondence to find.

"Did you find anything else that might be interesting?" Tj asked

"Not about the fire, but maybe about the extra body in the coffin," Kyle answered.

"Okay, so what did you find out?"

"The original occupant of the coffin was a woman named Estella Goodwin. She died shortly after the incident with the fire. She was an elderly woman who died of natural causes. At the time of her funeral, as you know, her granddaughter slipped her favorite necklace into the coffin with her grandmother's body. The burial was scheduled for later the same day, but a torrential downpour flooded the cemetery.

The family made the decision to hold off on the burial and returned the body to the funeral home after the church service. Two days later, the coffin was buried. Initially, I was working under the assumption that the coffin was dug up and the second body was placed inside at some later point, but what if the second body was added before the burial?"

"Don't you think someone would have realized that?" Mike asked. "Even if they didn't look inside, the coffin would have been a lot heavier with two bodies."

"What if someone from the funeral home, or perhaps the cemetery, was in on the addition of the second body?" Kyle asked.

"Why would anyone agree to do something like that?" Ben asked.

Kyle shrugged. "It's an easy way to make a few bucks. Someone comes along and needs a body hidden. They offer to pay a pretty penny to have it placed in a coffin. What's the harm? Who would ever know?"

"Makes sense," Tj agreed. "If the girl hadn't slipped the necklace into the coffin with her grandmother, chances are no one would ever have known about the second body. So what's the point again?"

"The point is," Kyle began, "that if that's what occurred we have a timeline for searching missing persons reports. If the coffin was randomly dug up and the second body had been placed inside, it could have happened at any time after Estella was buried, but if the body was added during the two days between the funeral and the burial, it narrows the field quite a bit."

"So can you pull up the missing persons reports from that time period?" Tj asked.

"I can but I think it will be quicker and easier to ask Roy or Tim to do it. I'll go by and talk to them about it tomorrow. It's just a hunch but I have a feeling that identifying the second body might provide a valuable clue as to what is going on here.

"Agreed. I'll go by the funeral home and see if I can find out what the current owner thinks might have happened all those years ago," Tj offered.

CHAPTER 4

Later that evening, Tj sat in the resort bar with Hunter. They were both exhausted, but they'd barely seen each other during the past week of snowmageddon and felt the need to catch up. The Lakeside Bar and Grill had reopened for regular service that day, but most of the guests were curled up inside next to the fireplaces that were provided in every cabin and lodge room.

"I ran into Jake today," Tj began as she nibbled on the chicken wing she found herself picking at. "He was coming into the hospital while I was going out after visiting with Stella."

"He must have been on his way for his physical therapy appointment."

"How's he doing with that?" Tj wondered.

Jake Hanson was Tj's favorite member of the Hanson clan next to Hunter. He'd suffered a mild stroke a couple of months before and since then, he'd been required to adhere to a strict diet and exercise regimen.

"Honestly, not so well. I'm doing everything I can to make sure he does the exercise he's supposed to be doing each day, but having to monitor his every move has turned me into a huge nag and him into a grouchy old man."

"I'm sorry to hear that." Tj had always appreciated Jake's easygoing personality. "Can I help?"

"Sure, if you want to go with him to his next physical therapy session, find out what he's supposed to do, and then make sure he does it," Hunter said sarcastically.

"Okay."

Hunter paused and looked at her. "Really? You would do that?"

Tj shrugged. "Sure. I went through it with my grandpa after he had his stroke. It was hard, but he got through it, and as a result of my nagging, he's pretty much back to his old self."

"I'd love to push this off on you, but I feel bad about even considering doing so. He's my grandfather, and I'm a doctor. I should be used to dealing with difficult patients."

"He's not your patient; he's family," Tj reminded him. "You love him. It's not easy to try to make someone you love do something they don't want to do. Let me try working with him. Jake is a strong man, and with a little encouragement from someone who isn't his grandson he might do just fine. When's his next therapy session?"

"Monday afternoon."

"What time?"

"Four."

Tj frowned. "The girls have dance on Mondays, and I have downhill practice until three. I can probably drop them off if you can pick them up."

"If you'll tackle Grandpa for even one day for me I'll happily take the girls to dance *and* pick them up. In fact, I'll just pick them up from school. I should be done at the hospital by then, barring any emergencies. I'll take them to get a snack before dance."

"Okay." Tj smiled. "You have a deal."

The pair shook hands across the table.

"And please be sure that each sister has her hat, gloves, and jacket before you leave the school grounds."

"Did you ever find Gracie's jacket?" Hunter asked.

Tj had vented to Hunter after she'd come home from school with yet another piece of clothing missing.

"No, not yet. I'm sure it's long gone. Jenna told me Grainger's has jackets on sale. I'm going to stop off to buy one tomorrow. If she loses this one, I don't know what I'm going to do. Being a single mom is expensive."

"Maybe you should talk to Jordan about helping out," Hunter suggested.

Tj's mom had named her legal guardian of her younger half-sisters before she died. It was a role she'd been unprepared for but happy to take on, even though at times she felt that she was hanging on to her sanity by a thread. The previous Christmas, a man named Jordan Tanner had shown up claiming to be Gracie's biological father. Although they hadn't yet taken the step of conducting a paternity test, it seemed likely that Jordan was indeed her father. A captain in the Navy, Jordan planned to retire and move to Serenity to be near Gracie in the summer.

"I've thought of that, but I still think of Gracie as being mine. I think Jordan respects that, at least for the time being, and I don't want to do anything that might alter the paradigm. Besides, I like to complain, but I have enough money to buy Gracie a coat or whatever else she needs. Even with the losing stuff situation, she's still the easier of the sisters to deal with most of the time."

"Ashley still mooning over the new boy in her class?"

Tj rolled her eyes. "It's like a soap opera every day with that girl. She's only in the fourth grade. I really thought I had a couple more years before I had to deal with broken hearts and backstabbing best friends."

"There's a backstabbing best friend now?" Hunter asked as he took a sip of his beer.

"I guess I never had the chance to fill you in. Apparently, the boy Ashley claims she is deeply in love with has a thing for Kristi. It all started when..."

Tj continued to fill Hunter in on the drama that was currently being played out in Serenity Elementary School's fourth grade classroom. At times like this she felt like she and Hunter were best girlfriends laughing and chatting about their day. They'd been in each other's lives since they were in elementary school themselves, and it felt comfortable to confide in him the same way she did in Jenna. She loved Hunter and considered him to be one of her best friends, and most of the time she was happy with that. And then there were other times when she caught his eye and remembered the passion they'd once shared and was certain she wanted what he did: something more.

"And then," Tj laughed, "Ashley leaned over and kissed this poor kid square on the lips in front of the entire class."

"Oh, no." Hunter laughed. "What did he do?"

"He kissed her back and then ran out the door. I was supposed to go talk to Ashley's teacher about her inappropriate behavior, but the storm arrived, delaying the meeting, so I have that to look forward to."

"Lucky you." Hunter grinned.

"Yeah." Tj suddenly realized that she *was* lucky to have Ashley and all of her preteen drama in her life. "Lucky me."

"Did Kyle get any new information about Nolan's death from the computer and files?" Hunter asked.

Tj filled him on the paperwork and computer reports Kyle had found in Nolan's office.

"It sounds like digging into this case could be dangerous," Hunter pointed out. "Maybe it would be a good idea to let the folks at the sheriff's office handle this. I don't want you getting hurt."

"Nolan was family. I'm not going to get hurt, and I'm not going to drop it."

"I figured, but at least I can say I tried. How can I help?"

"At this point I'm not sure what you can do, but I'll definitely let you know if something comes up."

Hunter finished his beer and ordered another before he continued. "Grandpa and I were talking about the old arson case this morning. He said that most folks thought it was odd they let Clay Warner go after the second fire. Most felt he was guilty of killing the young couple, and a second fire using the same signature didn't necessarily negate that."

Tj considered this. "Based on the information Kyle has managed to dig up, there were some very specific and unique aspects to the fire that killed the young couple that were kept secret at the time and never made public. The argument that Warner's attorney made was that for the second fire to likewise exhibit those same unique qualities, both fires must have been set by the same person. His client was in lockup at the time of the second fire, so he couldn't have set *either* fire."

"Did Nolan's notes indicate what was so unique about the two fires?" Hunter asked.

"Kyle is still looking through all the notes, but he hasn't found an explanation so far."

"Maybe Warner had a partner who knew exactly how to duplicate the first fire," Hunter suggested.

"I thought of that. It would help if we could talk to someone who was involved in the case at the time. Maybe Judge Harper."

Harold Harper was a retired judge and the current mayor of Serenity. He had also been a good friend of Nolan's.

"I guess it couldn't hurt to ask him. He was most likely the bench judge at the time. I suppose there might have been more going on than it appears on the surface if the district attorney dropped the case so readily." Hunter glanced at his watch. "I know if feels like the middle of the night, but it's really still pretty early. I can call him if you'd like."

"Yes, let's," Tj agreed.

Luckily, Judge Harper was both at home and willing to speak to them. He was a good friend of Tj's Grandpa Ben and Hunter's Grandpa Jake, so Tj and Hunter both knew him well.

Judge Harper lived on a lakefront estate just outside of town. Although Tj was exhausted, she decided they really should pay him a visit that evening, when they had the opportunity. Who knew what the next few days would bring? Hunter, who'd never drunk his second beer, offered to drive and then return Tj to the resort when they were done.

The drive from the highway to the house was almost half

a mile and Tj was concerned that it might not have been plowed, but when they arrived at the gate they were greeted with a road that was in better shape than most in town. Tj guessed you received first dibs on plow service when you were the mayor of the town.

"Hunter, Tj, so nice to see you. Do come in," Judge Harper greeted them. "Would you like something to drink?"

"We just came from the Grill, so we're fine," Hunter answered for both of them.

"We don't want to take up a lot of your time," Tj began, "but we did have a few questions we hoped you could answer."

"Certainly; come on back. I have a fire going in the study."

Judge Harper showed Tj and Hunter to a small room at the back of the house that was lined with bookcases and contained a desk and a chair, as well as a sofa and a flat-screen television. He indicated that they should have a seat on the sofa while he sat down behind the desk.

"So how can I help you?" he asked.

"I guess you heard about Nolan," Hunter began.

Judge Harper bowed his head. "Yes, I heard."

"And I'm sure you can guess that Tj has been snooping around, trying to find the killer," Hunter teased in an effort to lighten the mood.

Judge Harper smiled sadly. "I figured."

"We had some questions about Clay Warner and the fire he may or may not have set that killed that young couple." Tj decided to take control of the conversation. "We figured you were on the bench when the case was first heard."

"Actually, Judge Silverstone was on the bench when the

case against Mr. Warner was first brought forward. I had taken a sabbatical in order to deal with the death of my wife. I was in town, however, so I have a rudimentary knowledge of what went on."

Tj knew that Judge Silverstone had passed away a few years back.

"Was Boggs sheriff then?" Tj wondered.

"No, Boggs didn't become sheriff until Sheriff Tolly passed away, a year or so after Clay Warner was released."

"Here's the thing," Tj began. "Grandpa and I were talking, and we have reason to believe that Nolan may have been killed as a result of getting too close to something in one of the cold cases he was working on. According to Grandpa, he had several irons in the fire, including the dropped case against Clay Warner. We're here in the hopes that you might be able to shed some light on exactly what went on at the time the whole thing was happening."

Judge Harper sat quietly, looking at the pair. It appeared to Tj that he was trying to make up his mind about whether to share what he knew. He was no longer a judge, nor did he currently work in the justice system, but he was the mayor, even if in Serenity the mayor held more of an honorary title, and most likely felt an obligation to avoid discussing confidences that weren't his to share.

"Clay Warner was what most folks referred to as a bad seed. He was born to an alcoholic mother who raised him on her own after his father left town when he was just a baby. He had a police record by the time he was twelve and was in and out of the juvenile justice system until he turned eighteen, when he was driving drunk and was involved in a hit and run that left a woman permanently paralyzed. He was sent to prison, where he served out his term. While he was in prison his mother froze to death while passed out under the decking of one of the old boathouses in the area."

"Oh, no. How sad," Tj sympathized. "And how difficult for Warner to have his mother die while he was locked up."

"He was understandably angry," Judge Harper confirmed.

"So how did he end up back in Serenity if his mother had passed?" Hunter asked.

"After he was released from prison Warner returned to town with the intention of living in the childhood home his mother had promised would be his when she died. He found the young couple who were later killed in the fire living in the house. It seemed the mother had failed to pay her mortgage for months before she passed, the bank had repossessed the house and the land it sat on, evicted his mother who then became homeless, and sold it to the young couple while he was away."

Suddenly, Tj realized exactly where the story was going.

"He blamed both the bank and the couple who bought the house for his mother's death and his homelessness," Judge Harper continued. "He publically threatened them several times before they perished in the fire. Everyone was certain Clay Warner had set the fire, and he was arrested almost immediately. Clay insisted from the beginning that he was innocent, but he didn't have an alibi for his whereabouts at the time of the fire."

Judge Harper took a sip of his scotch before he continued. "A week or so after his arrest, I started to hear some chatter that the arrest had been mishandled, and that due to errors made during the process the district attorney was questioning his ability to prosecute the case. The conversations that were conducted regarding this very sensitive case took place behind closed doors, and since I was on leave, I could only pick up bits and pieces. I'm not sure what would have ended up happening because several days later there was a second fire. No one was harmed, but the specific method used to ignite the second blaze mimicked the first exactly. Clay's attorney argued that he couldn't have started the second fire because he was locked up, and because the first and second fires appeared to have been set by the same person he was therefore innocent of both."

"So they released him," Tj finished.

The judge nodded his head.

"Do you know what happened to him?" Tj asked.

"He disappeared as soon as he was released. As far as I know, no one has seen him since."

"I suppose moving on was a good idea. It sounds like he wasn't very popular," Tj said.

"People in the area not only didn't like him, they didn't trust him. It's my opinion that if the initial arrest hadn't been botched the district attorney might not have allowed him to be released in spite of the second fire. Actually, whoever set the second fire did both the sheriff's office and the district attorney's office a favor."

Tj frowned. "What do you mean?"

"The death of the young couple in the fire was a very emotional subject. If there had been an error during the arrest of Clay Warner that would have led to his eventually being released on a technicality, there would have been an uproar in the community that neither the sheriff nor the district attorney would have been able to come back from.

You need to keep in mind that Clay had grown up here. He'd hurt a lot of people during his short life. The woman he paralyzed in the hit and run was well liked."

"So there were people on the inside who could have set the second fire in order to cover up the initial mistake," Tj realized. "The details of the first fire might not have been made public, but those on the inside would have known about them."

"That has been my theory, and that's what I told Nolan— who, by the way, was a deputy at the time this all went down."

"You don't think Nolan was the deputy who made the mistake?" Hunter asked.

"No. We talked about it and it seemed clear it hadn't been his error, but he had his suspicions. A very public mistake that would have caused the release of such an unpopular and feared man would have virtually ended the career of the deputy who made it."

"So if the deputy wanted to protect his career he might have set the second fire so Clay would be released before the error could have become public knowledge," Tj restated.

"That was the theory Nolan was working from," Judge Harper confirmed.

"Do you know what the mistake was?"

"No, not specifically. I was on sabbatical so not really in the loop and the sheriff's office went out of their way to cover it up. If I had to guess, I'd say they either arrested Warren without legally obtained evidence or they forged evidence in order to make the arrest."

"So if the second fire was set by someone on the inside to cover up the mistake maybe Nolan was getting close to figuring out who set the second fire and he was killed before he could release the information," Tj speculated.

"Perhaps. But keep in mind that Nolan knew all the suspects. Even if the deputy who made the mistake set the second fire that resulted in Clay Warner's release, that doesn't mean that same person turned around and killed Nolan," Judge Harper cautioned.

"That's true, but it's a place to start, and Grandpa is certain Nolan knew the person who attacked him. How do we find out who the deputy was who made the mistake?" Tj asked.

"The original report has the name blacked out, but we know there were four deputies who responded to the fire. Nolan figured it was one of the four who made the mistake, although it's possible the error occurred during the incarceration process and not during the arrest," Judge Harper answered.

"And who were the four deputies who responded?" Tj asked.

"Dover Wood, Jerry Johnson, Max Stevens, and Jim Boggs."

"Sheriff Boggs?"

CHAPTER 5

Friday, March 13

Friday dawned bright and sunny, with temperatures that promised to climb into the forties. The walkways Mike and Tj had worked so hard to keep shoveled began to melt, and the guests who had booked cabins were allowed to return to them. Most of the businesses in town had reopened, and with the exception of the huge piles of snow that had been created by the plows, you'd never even know the storm of the decade has just blown through.

Tj found that she was torn when she realized she finally had a few hours to herself. She was dying to head up to the slopes to take advantage of the fresh powder, but she also wanted to follow up on the four names Judge Harper had provided the previous evening. Sheriff Boggs was exactly the type of man to make a mistake and then try to cover it up by committing a felony. He'd also had ambition to rise up in the ranks and therefore, of the four, seemed to have the most to lose. Her money was on him as the arsonist of the second fire, but she couldn't prove it and she certainly couldn't prove he'd killed Nolan.

Dover Wood still lived in the area. He'd left law enforcement shortly after the incident and now owned the local feed store. She remembered that Hazel had mentioned that Nolan had been seen in the feed store the day before the storm. Maybe he had been investigating the cold case, as Hazel had asserted. Tj didn't know Dover well, but she had chatted with him on a number of occasions when she went in to pick up dog food or order feed for the Maggie's Hideaway stables. She supposed she could use more dog food, which would give her an in to chat with the guy.

Jerry Johnson was still a deputy, although he worked out of the office in Indulgence. Tj didn't know the man well enough to simply call and start asking questions, but she was sure Roy must have spent some time with him in an official capacity, so she figured having a chat with Roy would be the best place to start.

Max Stevens had retired from the sheriff's office and now spent most of his time hanging out at the senior center. Nolan had also liked to hang out at there, as did Ben and Doc. Tj figured she could get an overview of the man from Ben and then decide how to proceed after that. She'd called Kyle earlier and he'd promised to nose around in each man's banking and phone records after he took his entourage of giggling girls to the movie he had promised Ashley he would both pay for and chaperone. By this point his list of *dates* for the matinee was up to ten. Kyle promised to meet with her when he returned from his excursion.

Tj knew Jenna had opened the Antiquery now that the storm had passed, Hunter and Doc were at the hospital helping with the transfer of patients down the mountain now that the road had reopened, and her dad and grandpa were busy at the resort, which left her clean out of partners in crime, at least for the morning.

After considering her options Tj decided to strap on some snowshoes and take the two adult dogs for a walk to stretch their legs. She needed to clear her mind, and she was sure that Gracie, who had opted not to go with the older girls, would be happy to keep her eye on the puppies. One of the most awesome things about living at Paradise Lake was that it could be storming one day and sunny and warm the next. By the time Tj had traveled just a quarter mile down the beach she'd discarded her sweatshirt and tied it around her waist.

The storm had left in its wake a clear blue sky and an even bluer lake. The contrast of the deep blue with the white of the freshly fallen snow brought tears to Tj's eyes as she considered how very lucky she was to live in such a beautiful setting. Echo and Kai were having the time of their lives plowing through the deep powder as the forest animals began to emerge from their shelters and make their way down to the lake.

Tj paused to look out over the clear glassy water. She still couldn't believe Nolan was really gone. He'd been a part of her everyday life for so long that she knew that his absence would create a hole not easily filled. She remembered how he always entered the hottest chili in the annual chili cook-off, and how he'd entered his famous pork ribs in the barbecue cook-off each summer. He'd helped her solve Tonya Overton's murder just last summer and was always around when she really needed him.

Tj wiped the tears from her cheeks as she continued on. There were some people in the world who simply were not replaceable, and Nolan was one of those people.

She was tired, and there was a part of Tj that simply wanted to climb into her big bed, pull the down comforter over her head, and sleep until she had to go to work on Monday. But another part of her, a bigger part, wanted to find out who'd killed Nolan and make sure that person was brought to justice.

Tj couldn't help but play the facts she had gathered so far over in her mind. She was becoming more and more certain that his death had to be related to one of the cold cases he'd been working on. Nothing else made sense. Nolan was a nice guy who was liked and respected by everyone in the community. Tj couldn't think of a single reason that anyone would want the man dead unless he was getting close to uncovering a truth that someone wanted to remain buried.

Tj pushed her body to its limit as she tried to work off her anger as well as her grief. Trying to figure out who had killed Nolan when she really didn't have any clues to work with was going to get her nowhere, so she decided to try to focus on something else. Something happy and comforting, like puppies. Kai's puppies sure were cute. They'd been terrorizing the house since the moment she brought them home, but they were also soft and funny and so sweet to snuggle with. Echo loved them, and Gracie was in her element as substitute mom. Tj knew it was going to be hard on her little sister when it was time for them to leave, but as far as she knew Stella had already promised all three puppies to people who had applied to provide them with forever homes.

Which brought Tj's thoughts to Stella and the uncertainty of her situation. As badly as she wanted to bring Nolan's killer to justice, she wanted Stella to wake up and return to her life even more. Realizing that she was never going to achieve the inner peace she longed for when there were so many things causing her stress, Tj turned around and headed back toward the resort. Her body was tired, but her mind was even more restless. By the time she showered and dressed she figured she'd have time to stop by the funeral home before it would be time to meet Kyle.

The Serenity Funeral Home had changed ownership several times over the years, so Tj held out little hope that anyone who worked at the home at the time Kyle hypothesized the second body might have been placed in the coffin with the dead woman would still be around, but she figured it couldn't hurt to ask. The current owner had purchased the business from the previous owner a good ten years ago, but Tj thought she'd heard that the new owner was one of the employees of the previous owner.

"Can I help you?" A tall thin woman asked after Tj walked in through the front door and rang the bell on the counter.

"My name is Tj Jensen. I was hoping to speak to the owner."

"If you are here to make arrangements for a loved one I can help you with that."

"No, it's not that. I had some questions of a personal nature." Tj glanced at a stack of business cards on the counter identifying the owner by name. "Is Jeff in?"

"He is working from home today. I suppose if you know him you can call him there."

"Okay, I will." Tj didn't want to admit that she had no idea where the man lived so she picked up one of his business cards and figured she'd check the phone directory. "Have you worked here long?" Tj asked.

"Four years."

Not long enough, Tj realized. "Okay, well thank you for your time and have a nice day."

After Tj left the funeral parlor she looked at the business card in her hand. There was a phone number under the name Jeff Everley, but Tj suspected the phone number was connected to the funeral home. Her dad knew a lot of people in town so she called him to find out if he knew Jeff and if he might know where he lived.

"Hey dad," Tj said once Mike picked up his cell. "Do you know the new owner of the funeral home? His name is Jeff Everley."

"Yeah, I know Jeff. He used to bowl with the league I bowled with a couple of years ago."

"I wanted to ask him about the second body in the coffin but the woman I spoke to at the funeral home said he was working from home."

"If Kyle is correct in his theory that the second body was added to the coffin during the two days between the woman's funeral and burial Jeff won't be able to help you. He didn't move to the area until several years later. I've actually been mulling the idea over ever since Kyle suggested it. A man named Jacob Louder owned the funeral home at the time Estella Goodwin was buried. It was a family owned and operated business. Jacob died a few years after Estella was buried and his son Kent took over. Kent operated the business for a few years before deciding to sell to Jeff, who was a relatively new employee. The only person who might have been around when Estella was buried who is still around now is the groundskeeper whose name I can't seem to remember."

"Okay thanks dad. That helps. There is no use me tracking down a man who wasn't even here at the time we suspect the second body was buried. I'm supposed to meet up with Kyle. We'll catch up later. If you think of anything call or text. I really want to find whoever did this to Nolan."

"Will do. And you be careful. Whoever did this is obviously dangerous, and if it does turn out to be someone Nolan knew it might also be someone you know. Be careful of who you trust."

Kyle lived in a large house on a huge lakefront estate that had been left to him by Tj's good friend Zachary Collins, the grandfather Kyle never even knew existed. Tj had first met Kyle a year and a half earlier, when he'd stayed at the resort at the time of his grandfather's death. They'd bonded over their shared grief and had been the best of friends ever since.

Along with the house, Kyle had inherited Zachary's millions. He was by far the wealthiest man in the area, but Kyle remained a modest man who shared what he had and never let his wealth, or the power that seemed to come with it, go to his head. Tj had been an only child during her childhood, but her relationship with Kyle gave her a glimpse of what having a brother must be like. She loved Kyle and counted on him, but she didn't have romantic feelings for him, which was good because in Tj's experience, love of the romantic sort was hard and confusing and at times, best avoided entirely.

Tj let herself in through the front door and headed back toward the clean room where Kyle kept his computer equipment. The house had changed a lot since Zachary had lived there. Kyle had replaced most of the old and worn furniture and had hired a local contractor to carry out an extensive remodel that included new windows, flooring, and wall coverings. Tj's favorite part of the remodel was the kitchen. Although she didn't cook, she enjoyed sitting at the Italian marble counter sipping Kyle's expensive wine while he whipped them up one of his delicious meals.

In addition to the cosmetic changes Kyle had had made, he'd also updated the electrical system to handle the dozens of computers he kept on the premises. Kyle had been a computer programmer before coming into his inheritance, and he continued to dabble in the industry even though he no longer needed the money a steady job provided.

"How's the hunt going?" Tj asked when she joined Kyle in the computer room.

"Slowly. I did, however, find something interesting in the banking records of the four men we're now referring to as our prime suspects."

Tj had called Kyle earlier to fill him in on her conversation with Judge Harper. They'd agreed that if one of the deputies who had responded to the first fire had botched the arrest, they'd have motive to want to hush Nolan up if he was close to proving that the second fire had been set as a cover-up.

"Dover Wood, Jerry Johnson, Max Stevens, and Sheriff

Boggs all recently made large cash withdrawals from their savings accounts within a few weeks of one another," Kyle informed her.

"How large?" Tj asked.

"Between five and ten thousand dollars. Because they simply removed the cash from the bank there's no way to know how the money was spent, but none of the men withdrew large amounts of cash on a regular basis, so I found it interesting."

"Interesting, yes, but is it relevant?"

"I don't know," Kyle admitted. "My first thought was that the men were being blackmailed, but it doesn't make sense that all four men would be susceptible to blackmail if only one of the deputies who responded to the fire botched the arrest."

"Yeah, and even if they were all somehow in on it together, a blackmail scheme would almost assuredly point to Nolan as the blackmailer because he's the one who's dead, and I don't see him doing something like that."

"Yeah, me neither. Besides, it seems like if you were blackmailing four men for a single incident you'd blackmail them all for the same amount of cash."

"So maybe the withdrawals are nothing more than a coincidence," Tj decided. "Did you find anything else?"

"Not in their banking records. As for their phone records, Sheriff Boggs doesn't have any other than those associated with his work phone."

"What do you mean he doesn't have any phone records?" Tj asked.

"He doesn't have a landline connected with his home residence and there's no cell phone under his name. My guess is that when he isn't working he uses a burner phone. Given the sensitive nature of his job, combined with his tendency to annoy people, it may be for personal safety reasons rather than an attempt to cover anything up. Either way, I'm afraid looking at phone records for him is a dead end."

"And the others?"

"I didn't find any activity that jumped out at me as being suspicious. I looked at Nolan's phone records and didn't see anything that looked suspect on the surface, although there was a call made from his cell phone shortly after the one he made to your grandpa was terminated."

Tj frowned. "Who was the call to?"

"It was the public use land line in Murphy's Bar that is provided for times when the cell towers are out. The call lasted less than five seconds."

"Why would Nolan call the community line?"

"I don't know. Maybe he didn't. Maybe the killer used Nolan's phone to call the community phone at Murphy's."

"Why would the killer do that? It makes no sense."

"I agree. I'm just sharing what I found."

"Maybe Murphy can remember who was in the bar during the time the call was made," Tj hoped.

"I guess it wouldn't hurt to ask. Besides, after my *date* this morning I could use a drink."

"Was it that bad?" Tj asked as they began the process of putting on coats, boots, hats, gloves, and scarves.

"It was fun. And loud. And I know more about all the teen heart throbs than I ever wanted to know. I had no idea the boy crazies started at such a young age."

"With all the television shows focused on teenagers, kids

get a lot of access to who's hot and who's not. It's important to keep up with the trends if you want to hang with the cool crowd."

"Guess I'll have to pay more attention." Kyle laughed. "I was totally out of my league today. Speaking of who's hot, it looks like the shoot for the commercial is on for tomorrow. Are you still going to be able to help me?"

Tj knew how important the ad was to both Kyle and the town. "Absolutely. What's the plan?"

"We're going to meet the actors and crew at ten. First we're going to head up to Angel Mountain Ski Resort. After we get a few shots of them skiing we'll head back into town and get shots of them ice skating, sledding, and snowmobiling. Once we finish the outdoor scenes we're planning to get a few shots of them walking through town, as if they're shopping, followed by a dinner scene at the Beef and Brew."

"Sounds like a full day," Tj observed.

"It will be. Andrea said she could stay through the weekend, so if we have to we can get some of the shots on Sunday. I figured we'd start with the skiing and then do the ice skating. If necessary, we can shoot the sledding and snowmobiling the next day. Andrea has been extremely accommodating, especially considering the fact that she's been stuck in town all week with nothing to do."

"And has her costar been equally accommodating?" Tj asked. Brad was a total babe, but he seemed like the type who could be a huge prima donna.

"He's been considerably less accommodating, but Andi has assured me that he's a professional who will come through in the end."

"Andi?" Tj grinned.

"She told me that her friends call her Andi."

"And you're a friend?"

Kyle actually blushed. "We have spent some time together this week."

"Do I detect an interest of the romantic kind?" Tj teased.

"Of course not. The woman is doing the town a huge favor, and as a member of the town council I felt it my duty to see that she was entertained. Besides, she's leaving on Monday and I'll most likely never see her again. Now can we go to Murphy's?"

Tj just laughed at his obvious discomfort. In all the time she'd known Kyle, she'd never noticed him noticing a woman. At least not in *that* way.

Murphy's was mostly deserted on weekday afternoons. Although Murphy sold food, people came to the bar to drink rather than eat. There was a four top in the back where the guys from Chamberlain Construction were hanging out, and there were three men sitting on barstools watching a golf tournament on the television behind the bar. Kyle and Tj sat down in a booth away from the others and waited for Murphy to come by to take their order.

"What can I getcha?" Murphy asked.

"I'd like a glass of Chardonnay," Tj answered, "but first I wanted to ask if you remember anyone calling into the community phone on Wednesday?"

"Not off hand. Why do you ask?"

"We have reason to believe that the call could be a clue in Nolan's murder."

"I wish I could help you. Nolan was a good guy. One of the best. But we were the only place in town to get food or a drink and we were slammed the entire day. In fact, we were slammed the entire week. To be honest, it's all a big blur. I can barely remember one day from the next, let alone a specific point in time."

"Do you remember if Sheriff Boggs was in on Wednesday?" Tj asked.

"No. I haven't seen him all week. I doubt he came around the lake with the storm and all. I hear there were as many accidents on the south shore as there were up on this end of the lake."

"How about Jerry Johnson or Dover Wood?"

Murphy thought about it. "I haven't seen Jerry since he transferred to the main office, and I can't say as I remember seeing Dover that day either. But like I said, a huge blur. I'm really sorry. It's completely possible there were people here I didn't even notice."

"Can you think of anyone you did see that afternoon?" Kyle asked. "Just because you didn't see who answered the phone doesn't mean someone else didn't spot him."

"Lots of folks who live close by came in." Murphy squinted as he tried to remember what he might know. "There was a basketball game on Wednesday that everyone wanted to see. I remember a group of guys rooting for their favorite team from the tables in the front of the bar, and there was a table of folks from the senior center in that back booth. The guys from the Chevron station down the street came in after they decided to close. I had a bunch of overflow from the Inn, and the gals from the hair salon shared a couple of pitchers. Like I said, it was packed."

"Okay, thanks," Tj said. "If you happen to remember anything odd, or if you can think of who might have been sitting in that booth near the phone, call me."

"Brandon Halliwell," Murphy said.

"Brandon answered the phone?" Tj asked.

"No, but he was sitting at that back table with Jeff Warren, Rob Riley, Hank Hammond, and a couple of others. Although, come to think of it, he might have come in later than the time you described." Murphy sighed. "I wish I could be more help. If I'd known what was going to happen I would have taken notes."

"It's okay," Tj reassured him. "I know how it is when you're in the midst of a crowd demanding service. I wouldn't have remembered either. If something does come to you, please call me."

"Will do. Drinks are on the house."

Tj and Kyle discussed a strategy while they sipped their beverages. Brandon Halliwell owned half of Guns and Roses, the ammo store/flower shop, with his sister Rita. Jeff Warren owned Warren Automotive, Hank Hammond owned the Beef and Brew, and Rob Riley was the owner of Rob's Pizza. It wasn't a lot to go on, but it was something, so Kyle and Tj decided to pay a visit on all four men.

They split up the list, with Tj going to talk to Brandon Halliwell and Rob Riley, while Kyle stopped by to chat with Jeff Warren and Hank Hammond. They arranged to meet at the Antiquery after they'd each completed their interviews.

Brandon and Rita Halliwell had inherited the space where Guns and Roses was located from their father, who had owned and operated Halliwell Guns and Ammo. Rita had wanted to use her half of the building to open a flower store.

Initially, Halliwell Guns and Ammo and Rita's Roses were marketed as two separate entities, but after everyone in town started calling the place Guns and Roses they'd decided to go with it and officially changed the name.

The interior of Guns and Roses was very much segregated, however. When you walked in through the centrally located front door you found guns and ammo to the right and flowers and potted plants to the left. Tj was willing to bet Brandon's was one of the best-smelling ammo stores in the country.

"Afternoon, Rita," Tj greeted when she entered the building. Brandon was helping a customer, so she decided to chat with the woman, who didn't appear to be busy. "How are things going in the flower industry?"

"Slow."

"Guess most folks are more focused on the snow than adding fresh flowers to their tables."

"It's just as well. I haven't been able to get any fresh stock for over a week. If you're here looking for flowers for the resort I'm afraid I won't have anything until I can get some shipped up from the valley."

"Actually, I'm here to speak to Brandon."

"He shouldn't be long. Guess you must be looking into Nolan's death."

"I'm helping out where I can."

"I was so sorry to hear about Nolan. He was one of the good ones. He'll be missed."

"Yes," Tj agreed, "he will."

"Have you heard whether the sheriff's office has any suspects?"

"I think they have a few angles they're exploring and

several people they're following up on, but as far as I know, they don't have anything really solid at this point."

"The whole thing is absurd. Who would want to kill Nolan? He was such a nice guy. Even when he was a cop he was known as being someone who treated people fairly and with respect."

Tj shrugged. "I wish I knew who was responsible, but right now I'm as stumped as anyone."

"If I hear anything I'll call you," Rita promised. "It looks like Brandon is done with his customer. Let me know if there's anything at all I can do. I should have fresh flowers in a day or two. I'd like to donate some for the funeral."

"Thanks. I'm not sure who's making the arrangements, but I'll be sure to let them know when I find out."

Tj looked toward the counter on Brandon's side of the store, where he was ringing up the customer he had been speaking to. Talk about a change of environment.

Rita's half of the store normally contained beautiful floral displays and scented candles, whereas Brandon's was decorated with animal heads and guns on display. Tj wasn't a huge fan of the animal heads and usually avoided the gun side of Guns and Roses, but if Brandon had any information at all to share, it would be worth venturing into the hunters' haven.

"What can I do for you?" Brandon asked as Tj crossed the store. She explained about the call from Nolan's phone to the community phone at Murphy's after Ben had overheard a struggle.

Brandon frowned. "I was at the bar that day a couple of different times. I left several times to check on things at the store, so I might have been gone at the specific time you mentioned." Brandon scratched his chin as he appeared to be considering the question. "I wish I could help you, but I was sitting with my back to the phone, and I don't remember noticing anyone using it."

"Who were you sitting with?" Tj asked.

"Jeff, Hank, Rob, Kurt, and Lloyd."

Kurt Brown was a local contractor and Lloyd Benson was a developer.

"Did you happen to notice if Sheriff Boggs or Jerry Johnson came in?"

"Didn't see them. Doubt they came around the lake with all the snow."

"How about Max Stevens or Dover Wood?"

"Max was with a group from the senior center, and I'm pretty sure I saw Dover sitting at the bar for a bit. Don't remember exactly when though. Might have been earlier in the day."

"Okay, thanks. By the way," Tj added, "Hazel told me Harriet said Nolan was in the store the day before the storm."

Brandon laughed. "Gotta love living in a small town. Everyone knows everyone else's business."

"That's true," Tj acknowledged. "I guess with everything that has happened I'm just curious why he was here. Hazel seemed to think he was investigating."

"Nolan wanted me to track down a gun for him. An old one he wanted to add to his collection. We were discussing the difficulties I might have tracking down that particular gun, and the cost of such a rare item. He insisted he really wanted that specific gun, so I agreed to look around to see what I could find."

"What kind of gun was he looking for?"

"An old Colt revolver. Hard to find but I told him I'd look."

"And were you arguing at any point in the conversation?" Tj asked.

"Not at all. Why do you ask?"

Tj shrugged. "You know how people like to talk. If anything comes to mind concerning the phone let me know."

"Will do."

Tj texted Kyle, telling him they needed to add Kurt Brown and Lloyd Benson to the suspect list, before heading down the street to Rob's Pizza. Kurt had worked on Kyle's remodel, so he volunteered to talk to him. Lloyd didn't live in Serenity, so he wouldn't be as easy to track down as the others.

Rob's was a comfy restaurant with vinyl booths, red-checkered tablecloths, team pictures on the walls, video games, and the best pizza west of the Rockies. Tj looked around. The place was packed, as usual. It appeared that a little bit of snow hadn't affected Rob in the least once he'd reopened after the storm.

"Hey, Tj. Want a booth?" Rob asked.

Normally, Tj loved coming to Rob's. Beside the fact that he made the best pizza around, Rob provided a cozy atmosphere, with a lived-in, hometown feel.

Somewhat off the beaten path, the eatery catered to locals rather than tourists, as many of the restaurants on the main drag were known to do. The walls were covered with photos of citizens going about their daily lives, winning contests, and receiving awards. Today, however, she was on a mission that didn't involve sampling the cheesy pies or ice-cold beer.

"No, thanks. I really just wanted to talk to you, if you have a minute."

"Yeah, okay. Come on back to the kitchen. I need to make a couple of pies for table eight. What's up?"

Tj explained about the phone call that had been made to Murphy's community phone and the potential importance of the call in tracking down Nolan's killer. "Did you notice anyone hanging around the phone?" Tj asked.

"Sure. Lots of folks. The phone is near the bathrooms, so people were going back and forth all day."

"Did you see anyone actually using the phone?"

Rob screwed up his face as he tried to remember. "It was really packed that day. There were folks just standing around drinking beer once all the tables filled up. The bathrooms were busy, but I'm not sure I remember anyone using the phone." Rob bit his lip as he spread grated cheese on the pie he was assembling. "I do remember that Hank said he left his phone at home and needed to make a call, but I think he just used Lloyd's." Rob began placing sliced pepperoni on the pizza. "You know, I do remember a phone ringing, now that I think about it. I remember figuring it was the phone Murphy keeps behind the bar, but I'm pretty sure it was the community phone. The community phone has an old-fashioned high-pitched ring, while Murphy's business line has more of a humming type of ringtone."

"Did you look up when you heard the phone?" Tj asked.

"Yeah. I do remember looking around the room. I wondered if it was someone's cell but then realized it sounded more like a landline."

"Try to remember if you saw anyone answer it," Tj encouraged.

Rob stopped what he was doing. He stared into space, as if he were trying to remember. "I was chatting with Jeff. I want to rebuild that old clunker my dad left me and was wondering if Jeff would help me with the project. He said he needed to use the can, so I refilled my glass and tried to pick up on the conversation the guys across from me were involved in. Kurt was talking to Hank about building a gazebo on the pier, behind his restaurant. I heard the ringing sound and looked around. Murphy was busy behind the bar, and no one seemed to be paying attention to the phone, which must have rung at least five times before someone picked it up."

"Can you remember anything about the person who picked it up?" Tj asked.

"I remember looking toward the bathrooms. Jeff was walking back toward the table. I was about to yell for him to catch the phone when one of the guys who was in line for the head picked it up. Wow." Rob looked surprised. "I didn't realize I saw all that."

"Do you know who picked up the phone?" Tj asked again.

"Some guy in a black hoodie. I didn't see his face. There was someone standing next to him who blocked my view."

"So the guy in the black hoodie was talking to someone while he waited for the bathroom?"

Rob scrunched his forehead. "The guy picked it up but then hung up right away. The person on the other end might even have hung up by the time the phone was answered. You know, I do seem to remember that Dover was in line for the john. Maybe he can provide more information."

Tj let out the breath she'd been holding. "Thanks, Rob.

Hopefully Dover knows who the guy in the black hoodie is."

Rob grinned. He looked proud of the fact that he'd been able to help. "Anytime. Hope you figure this out."

After Tj left Rob's she called Kyle to let him know she was heading over to the feed store. He confirmed that he'd spoken to Hank and Kurt, but Jeff had been with a customer when he'd stopped by, so he was planning to head back to the repair shop before meeting up with her at the Antiquery. Neither Hank nor Kurt seemed to know anything about a call to the community phone. Tj filled Kyle in on what she'd pried out of Rob. Rob had said Jeff had gone to the bathroom and was walking back to the table when the phone rang. Maybe he remembered who had been in line at the time.

CHAPTER 6

The feed store Dover Wood owned carried a little bit of everything animal related. Tj was able to purchase Echo's organic food through Dover, as well as order hay and grain for the horses in the stable. The store carried dog and cat toys and every type of leash, halter, and lead known to man, as well as supplies for fish, rabbits, birds, and pretty much any other type of animal one had a mind to domesticate.

"Afternoon, Tj. Special on dog food today."

"Actually, I do need dog food. I'll take a fifty-pound bag."

Dover began ringing up Tj's purchase.

"The main reason I stopped in was to ask you whether you were at Murphy's on Wednesday afternoon."

"Yeah, I was there."

"I don't suppose you remember standing in line for the bathroom when the community phone rang?"

"Darling, I don't remember the bathroom. Hope I made it. I have to admit I was so drunk that day I don't remember much. Why are you asking about the phone?"

Tj explained about the phone call that had been made from Nolan's phone. She watched his face for signs of guilt, but she supposed if he'd been at the bar he most likely wasn't their murder suspect, despite the fact that he was one of the four deputies Judge Harper had mentioned.

"Wish I could help. Nolan was a good guy, but I can't even remember who brought me home and put me to bed. The entire day is a total blur."

"Thanks. Let me know if you do think of anything."

Tj headed over to the Antiquery, where she had arranged to meet Kyle. She'd thought about asking Dover about the mistake that one of the deputies had made years ago but hadn't been sure exactly how to handle that delicate situation. She decided she needed a plan before she went ahead and risked blurting out the wrong thing.

As soon as she walked in the door she was hit with the most wonderful smell. The restaurant, which was only open for breakfast and lunch, was closed for the day by the time Tj arrived, but Jenna was busy baking bread and pastries to serve the following day.

"What's that smell?" Tj inhaled deeply as she removed her jacket.

"Chocolate croissants. Would you like one?"

"Would I like one? Of course I'd like one. They smell heavenly."

Jenna slid one, hot out of the oven, onto her plate. "I'm making these for a last-minute special order I got from Frannie Edison. She's hosting her book club tonight and needed a dessert to serve."

"I'm surprised the book club is even meeting with all the snow."

Jenna shrugged. "The plows have everything cleaned up, so I guess the seniors figured they might as well keep their plans. Dennis is finally off shift, so he's home with the girls. To be honest, staying here and baking in an empty restaurant sounded preferable to going home to sick kids. Not that I don't love my girls to pieces, but Dennis was happy to spend time with them because he really hadn't been able to hang out with them all week, and I was equally delighted for some peace and quiet after having been cooped up with them all week."

"Did your mom and Kallie go home?" Tj asked about the other two women who worked at the restaurant.

"Mom left early and Kyle took Kallie out to the resort to pick up Brady. Her car is acting up, so he was going to follow her over to Warren Automotive and then take her home. He said he'd be back when he was done, and he had news to share."

"I'm glad he has news, because I've been striking out. Kyle found out that someone used Nolan's phone to call the community line at Murphy's after the phone went dead while grandpa was talking to Nolan. We suspect the killer might have used Nolan's phone for some reason, although if that was what happened that was a dumb move on the killer's part. Anyway, I did manage to find out that someone in a black hoodie answered the phone at Murphy's when it rang, but I don't know who that person was. Rob seemed to think Dover Wood was near the phone when the man in the black hoodie answered it, but Dover said he doesn't recollect that. He admitted to having been very drunk after a full day of hanging out at the bar."

"Do you think he was lying?" Jenna asked. Tj took a bite of the pastry, then closed her eyes in ecstasy as the flaky pastry melted in her mouth.

She took a second bite before answering. "Why would he lie about being drunk?"

Jenna wiped her hands on the apron she had tied around her tall, slim form. "You said he was one of the four deputies who might have botched the arrest of Clay Warner. Maybe he wasn't really in line for the bathroom. Maybe he was waiting for the phone to ring and the other guy picked it up first."

Tj frowned. "I hadn't thought of that. Do you think he could have been working with someone?"

Jenna shrugged. She used the back of her hand to brush a wisp of her long blond hair out of her face. "I don't know. I don't know Dover all that well, but he seems like a nice guy. I guess it just occurred to me that his name has come up more than once." Jenna washed her hands and then tucked the hair that had come loose back up under her hairnet.

"That's true. Of the four men Judge Harper mentioned, two of them were seen at the bar: Dover Wood and Max Stevens. If you ask me, of the four, Dover and Max are the least likely to be the type to kill a man, but they do seem to have had opportunity, whereas no one remembers seeing either Sheriff Boggs or Jerry Johnson in town all week."

Jenna laughed. "It's funny that you suspect the two men who are still in law enforcement over the ones who are no longer cops."

"You've met Boggs."

"Yeah. He definitely has the disposition of someone who could be prone to violence. Taste this filling for the apricot bars. It tastes a little off to me, although I'm certain I made it the same way I always do."

Jenna used a clean spoon to scoop out a taste. She handed it to Tj.

"It's delicious," Tj said.

"I feel like my taste buds have been off lately, which is dangerous for a cook. I made spaghetti at home last week and everyone said it was too salty, but it didn't taste salty at all to me."

"The filling for the apricot bars is perfect. Take my word for it," Tj insisted. "Maybe you're coming down with the flu Kristi and Kari had."

"I hope not. I'm shorthanded at the restaurant this week as it is."

"Other than the taste-bud thing, have you been feeling okay?" Tj asked.

"Maybe a little run-down, but it's been hectic with Dennis working so much, the girls being sick, and all the snow."

Tj poured herself a cup of coffee as Jenna slid the apricot bars into the commercial oven. Not only did Jenna make the best pastries in town, she made the best coffee as well.

"Kristi was really disappointed that she missed going to the movies with Kyle and the gang this morning, but I hated to send her when she was just getting over being sick."

"Has she mentioned anything more about the situation with Ashley and the boy who seems to be getting in the way of their friendship?" Tj wondered. She'd tried to talk to Ashley about it, but her sister wasn't talking.

"Kristi swears she has no interest in this boy and insists she has done absolutely nothing to encourage his attention. She's both mad and hurt that Ashley is telling everyone that she's a backstabber."

"Poor Kristi," Tj sympathized. "I've tried to talk to Ashley, but I'm afraid she isn't being reasonable. She insists that the only reason this boy doesn't like her is because Kristi stole him away. I've tried to make her see that Kristi would never do that, but she's erected a wall on the subject that no one has been able to scale so far. I even asked Dad to talk to her, but he didn't get anywhere either. Ashley has had trouble interacting with people since she came to live with me after Mom died, but she's been best friends with Kristi since the day she moved here. Her stubbornness on this issue just doesn't make sense."

"Since when do nine-year-olds make sense? I'm sure it will blow over in a few weeks and they'll be back to being besties," Jenna reassured her.

"I hope so. Ashley is going to have a hard road in life if she can't learn to be a bit less combative about every little thing. I've been thinking about scheduling another movie day after Kristi begins to feel better, with both girls in attendance. Ashley adores Kyle. I have a feeling she won't want to look bad in front of him by acting petty."

"Could work," Jenna agreed. "On the other hand, Kristi has a bit of a crush on Kyle, so the date could end in bloodshed."

Tj groaned. "I'm really not sure I have what it takes to do this motherhood thing. Every single night when I go to bed I review my day and ask myself if I've made a lame decision that will scar one or both of the girls for life."

Jenna laughed out loud. "You really need to learn to relax. The girls are doing great. You love them and they know it. I promise that they'll grow up to be the awesome people you hope they will be. Besides, mothering is hard even for those of us who started with infants. When I told Kristi that I met Andrea Washburn she was so impressed, and she said that now that we had a personal connection to Hollywood she might quit school in a few years and become an actress."

"Yikes."

"Yikes is right. She has fan fever and thinks Andrea is the best thing to come along in forever, but it'll pass and she'll be on to the next preteen frenzy."

"So how did you meet Andrea Washburn?" Tj asked.

"She came in for lunch the day before the storm hit and we had to close," Jenna answered.

"How did she seem?"

Jenna slipped on mitts to check the items in the oven. "Actually, she was very nice. Really down to earth and approachable. She signed napkins for each of the girls."

"I think Kyle might be interested in her," Tj commented.

"Really? Why do you say that?" Jenna asked as she removed one of the trays from the oven.

"He's been showing her around, and when he mentioned spending time with her he got all red. I'm sure it's nothing serious, but it was fun to tease him about it."

"How do you know it isn't serious?"

"I doubt she's really his type."

"I wouldn't be so sure. She *is* really good-looking," Jenna pointed out.

"Yeah, but I doubt she has much depth under the glam."

"I don't know about that," Jenna countered. "She seemed very intelligent, and she had this girl-next-door quality about her. She stopped to chat with everyone who came up to her while she was here for lunch and she must have signed a couple dozen autographs. She was very gracious."

"Still, I doubt Kyle would be interested in a long-distance relationship," Tj said.

"People do it."

"People do what?" Kyle asked as he walked in from the alley. He stomped the snow off his boots before continuing on into the kitchen.

"Never mind."

"Coffee?" Jenna asked him.

"I'd love some. The temperature has dropped now that the sun is going down. It can't be more than two degrees out there."

"I heard it might get down to minus ten tonight, but it's supposed to be sunny and warm tomorrow." Jenna slid a cup of steaming coffee in front of Kyle.

"So what did you find out?" Tj asked. "I've been dying to hear your news because I all but struck out on my end."

Kyle took a sip of his coffee before answering. He sighed in relief as the warm liquid warmed him from the inside out. "I spoke to Jeff and asked him whether he'd noticed the person who had on the black hoodie when he returned from the bathroom," Kyle answered before taking a second sip. "He said he had, but he didn't get a good look at him other than that he was about the same height as Dover and had a slim build."

"So Dover was in line for the bathroom when the phone rang, like Rob thought," Tj concluded.

"That's what Jeff said. Why? Did Dover deny it?"

"He didn't deny it, but he said he was drunk and didn't remember anything. To be honest, I couldn't tell if he was lying or not. So, about the guy in the black hoodie...did Jeff notice hair color? Eye color? Anything that could help narrow it down?"

"No. He said he only glimpsed the guy as he walked past,

and he had the hood of his sweatshirt pulled over his hair. It also partially hid his face, but Jeff said he didn't seem familiar."

"The person in black could have been a visitor who got stuck in town when the storm hit," Jenna pointed out.

"Yeah, it could have happened that way," Kyle agreed.

"The real question is, who was the call intended for?" Tj asked.

"Maybe it was a misdial," Jenna speculated.

"Okay, then, who misdialed?" Tj wondered. "If things happened the way we suspect, the person who came to Nolan's door knocked him out and drug him to his car. One of two things had to have occurred; either Nolan came to and called Murphy's for some reason or the killer used the phone to make the call."

"Or the phone, which was found in Nolan's pocket, accidentally made the call when he was being dragged," Jenna volunteered.

"Grandpa said he was talking to Nolan and there was a knock at the door. Nolan set the phone down and answered it. He greeted the person, and then Grandpa heard a struggle. Then the phone went dead. It stands to reason that the person who knocked Nolan out turned off the phone. Why put it in his pocket?"

"I don't know why the killer would do that, but the phone got into his pocket somehow," Jenna said.

Tj nodded. "I suppose the call to the bar could have been a signal to someone that the deed was done. I still have no idea why the killer would have used Nolan's phone, but let's assume they had a reason to do so. The man in the black hoodie answered the phone, so he could have been an accomplice, unless Dover is lying and he was supposed to be the one to answer the phone and the other guy got to it first. I'll try working on Dover again. If he's lying about what went down, maybe I can trip him up. Even if he *was* drunk, the memory of that conversation must be buried somewhere in his subconscious. Maybe I can nudge it out of him."

"Sounds like a good next move," Kyle said.

Later that evening, after the girls had settled into their own rooms, Tj decided to try one more time to talk to Ashley about her feud with Kristi before she completely destroyed their relationship. The last time she'd broached the subject Ashley had been unwilling to even try to see Kristi's side of things, but more than a week had passed, so Ashley might have had a chance to think things through.

"All set?" Tj asked as she tucked the older of her two sisters into bed.

"Teeth are brushed, face washed, and clothes are in the hamper," Ashley confirmed.

Tj sat down on the bed next to Ashley. She tucked the covers up around her chin. "Did you have fun at the movie today?"

"It was okay." Ashley shrugged.

"And your friends all had fun?"

"I guess." She sighed.

"It's too bad Kristi was sick and had to miss out."

Ashley frowned but didn't say anything.

"I thought maybe Uncle Kyle would be willing to take you and Kristi to another movie when she's feeling better," Tj suggested.

"Kristi and me aren't friends anymore."

"I hope that's not true." Tj tucked a lock of Ashley's red hair behind her ear. "Jenna and I used to fight all the time when we were growing up, but we always made up, and now I have the best friend anyone ever had."

A single tear escaped Ashley's eye. "Kristi doesn't like me anymore."

"I'm sure that's not true." Tj stroked Ashley's hair while she struggled with her emotions.

"It is true. I was mad at her 'cause she liked stupid Porter, but she said she didn't, and I thought she was lying. I called her some bad words and she got mad, and I didn't care 'cause I was mad, but now I don't like Porter anymore 'cause he's a stupid head who didn't want to hang out with me, but Kristi is still mad that I called her bad names."

By this point tears were streaming down Ashley's face. Tj felt bad that Ashley was so upset, but she was glad she'd decided to have this talk with her. She had a feeling Ashley and Kristi would end up being lifelong friends like her and Jenna if they could make it through the trials of childhood.

"Have you tried apologizing to Kristi?" Tj asked.

"No. The storm came and there was no school. I haven't seen her, but when we went to the movie today Laura said she talked to Kristi, and Kristi is really mad and doesn't want to be my friend anymore." Ashley sobbed. "Laura said she only came to the movie 'cause Uncle Kyle was paying and she really wanted to see it, but she said she's on Kristi's side, so she won't be my friend anymore either." Ashley hiccupped. "And then the other girls said they liked Kristi too, and now I don't have any friends."

Ashley rolled over and buried her face in her pillow. Tj

gently rubbed her sister's back as she tried to figure out how to fix things.

Kristi tended to be a reasonable person who had forgiven Ashley on more than one occasion, so perhaps if she just got the girls together they'd work things out.

"How about I talk to Aunt Jenna about doing something with all four of us on Sunday if Kristi is feeling better? Maybe we could go to lunch or something."

"She won't want to come." Ashley sobbed into her pillow.

"She might. It wouldn't hurt to ask."

Ashley continued to cry.

"Is it at least okay if I call Aunt Jenna and talk to her about it?" Tj asked.

Ashley lifted her shoulder in a show of indifference.

"If Kristi is feeling better and she does want to go, do you think you're ready to apologize to her?"

Ashley rolled over and looked at Tj. "Do you think she'll come?"

"I'm not sure," Tj answered honestly. "Kristi is feeling bad that you called her bad names in front of all her friends, but maybe if you tell her you're sorry and you really mean it, she'll forgive you."

"Okay," Ashley agreed.

After checking on Gracie, who was sleeping on the floor with all five dogs, Tj called Jenna, who agreed to talk to Kristi. Unlike Ashley, who was a volcano of emotions ready to erupt at any moment, Kristi really was sweet and even-tempered, so Tj was confident they could work things out. Ashley had had a difficult time transitioning after the death of their mother and her move to Paradise Lake, but Kristi had stood by her through it all. Tj didn't know exactly what

Ashley had said about Kristi, but she hoped it wasn't so bad as to drive a permanent wedge between them.

Tj wandered downstairs and joined her dad and grandpa in the den, where the two men were watching an old western on TV.

"Girls settled in?" Mike asked.

"Seem to be. Gracie is sleeping on the floor again, but she has her warm footie jammies on, and I made sure she was on the mattress and under the covers."

"And Ash?" Mike asked.

"She's pretty upset about her fight with Kristi. She seems to be ready to apologize, so Jenna and I are thinking of taking the girls to lunch on Sunday. Initially, I was thinking about just taking Ashley and Kristi, but Jenna pointed out that the younger girls would provide a buffer, so I guess we're going to take all of them, as long as everyone is feeling okay."

"Ashley and Gracie seem to be over the sniffles they had," Ben commented.

"Yeah, and Jenna said her girls are doing better as well and should be fine to go to lunch by Sunday."

"I overheard you talking to Kyle on the phone earlier," Ben said, changing the subject. "I wanted to ask you if you had any news."

Tj filled her dad and grandpa in on everything they knew about Nolan's death to this point. It wasn't a lot, but it felt like a beginning.

"And I wanted to ask *you* about Max Stevens." Tj directed her question to Ben. "He was one of the four deputies to respond to the first fire, and I know he hangs out with the gang from the senior center."

"You think Max killed Nolan?" Ben sounded surprised.

"Not really, but I'm looking at every person whose name comes up. Of the four men who might have been motivated to cover up the mistake that was made during the first fire, Max seems to me to be the least likely, but he was at Murphy's the day the call came through from Nolan's phone."

"If Max was at the bar when Nolan was killed he couldn't have done it," Ben pointed out.

"That's true," Tj acknowledged. "Right now I'm operating under the assumption that there were at least two people involved: the person who was at Nolan's, killed him, and made the call, and the person at the bar, who the call was intended for."

"If you were going to kill someone and you wanted to let your partner know, why call him at all?" Mike asked. "Seems like an unnecessary risk."

Tj frowned. "That's true. Using Nolan's phone to make a traceable call to a public place makes no sense."

"Unless the phone call was a decoy," Mike suggested.

"Decoy?"

"How much time have you committed to figuring out who was on the receiving end of the call?" Mike asked.

"A lot," Tj admitted.

"It seems to me that the killer would be pretty dumb to use Nolan's phone to call the bar if his accomplice actually was at the bar and then leave the phone behind as proof that the call took place at all."

Tj sighed. Her dad had a point. A good point. The killer was either incredibly stupid or incredibly smart. Tj was afraid it was the latter.

CHAPTER 7

Saturday, March 14

Tj decided she needed to try to put Nolan's murder out of her mind for one day so that she could focus on the advertising campaign she'd agreed to help Kyle with. She was driven to find Nolan's killer, but she knew the campaign was important to Kyle, as well as to the town. And Maggie's Hideaway stood to benefit from the ad if it brought additional visitors to the area during the slower winter months. At least all the snow made everything look fresh and pristine. It was a sunny day, the lake was a deep royal blue, and the sky was crystal clear. The contrast of the blue sky and water and fluffy white snow was breathtaking. If Tj had to guess, the scenery that was shot that day was going to bring in droves of visitors on its own.

"Tj, I'd like you to meet Andrea, Brad, Grange, Kevin, and Josh," Kyle introduced her to the stars of the ad, as well as the crew who were along to produce and record the sequence of winter scenes. Grange was the director, and Kevin and Josh the cameramen.

"I'm happy to meet you all. It's a beautiful day to be on the slopes, and with all this fresh powder you should get some truly awesome shots."

"As I explained to Kyle earlier, neither Andrea nor Brad are skiers," Grange began. "He indicated that you have students with similar builds who can film the action shots?"

"Yes. They're going to meet us on the mountain," Tj answered. "Stephanie is tall and blond like Andrea, and Oliver is tall and dark-haired like Brad. They're both excellent skiers. I think they'll do well. They can ice skate too, if you need help with that too."

"Actually, that would be helpful. I don't want to risk either of my stars getting hurt. We can shoot your students and then take some close-ups of the actors to provide face shots. No one will ever know the difference."

Once the group arrived at the slope Kyle had arranged to use for filming, Grange explained to everyone exactly how he planned to get the shots he needed. Both Stephanie and Oliver were thrilled to be in the ad, and once wardrobe and makeup got done with them, you could barely tell them apart from the stars. Grange was a perfectionist who sent the pair up the hill several times so he could get shots from different angles. Tj was glad it worked out for Stephanie and Oliver to act as stunt doubles. They were great kids and seemed to be having the time of their lives.

"They're really good," Andrea commented at one point.

"They both have a shot at making the national team by the time they're seniors," Tj said proudly. "They've been boarding and skiing since they could walk. Kyle mentioned you used to live in the area. You never learned to ski?"

"I was only here for two years. I came to live with my

sister when our mom died. Then she also passed away, and I went to live with an aunt until I got my first modeling job."

"Wow, your mom and your sister both died within such a short period of time. I'm so sorry. That must have been really hard."

"Yeah, it was. I was really angry at first, and I'll admit I had a hard time getting on with my life, but when I found modeling it gave me a purpose."

"What made you decide to become an actress?" Tj asked.

"I didn't really plan to go into acting. I had a modeling gig that was part of a larger campaign that included television spots. The sponsor liked what I did and offered me a guest role in a television series they were producing and the rest is history."

"I'm happy it worked out. The people here are thrilled that such a big star would come to the area. I'm sorry our weather hasn't cooperated. I understand you were originally only supposed to be in town for a couple of days."

Andrea looked toward where Kyle was speaking to Grange. "It worked out okay. So what's the deal with Kyle? Are the two of you dating?"

"No," Tj said. "We're just friends."

"Is he single?"

Tj looked at Andrea. "Are you interested?"

Andrea shrugged. "He's very good-looking, and I hear he's filthy rich. He seems like the type who might be fun to party with. I leave for Paris next week. I was thinking about asking him if he wanted to come along."

Tj glanced at Kyle, who was now laughing at something Grange had said. "Kyle is single, but he's not unencumbered."

"What does that mean?"

"It means he has people in his life who depend on him. His mother lives in Serenity, and he has guardianship of a teenager who lives with his mother," Tj said shortly. "I suppose if you really are interested in Kyle you should ask him if he wants to go to Paris with you. It isn't my place to answer on his behalf."

Andrea continued to stare at Kyle. Her expression turned serious. "Thank you for your honest answer. I'll think about it. It looks like I'm up. See you later."

Tj couldn't help but notice Kyle noticing Andrea. She doubted he would be interested in chasing her around the world. On the other hand, he could certainly afford to do it if that was what he wanted, and his mom could look after Annabeth on her own. The thought of Kyle leaving didn't sit well with Tj at all. She wanted him to find that special someone, and she wanted him to be happy, but she also wanted him to find that person here, where she could hang out with him whenever she wanted. Was she being selfish? Absolutely. Did that change how she felt? Not in the least.

"So what do you think?" Kyle asked when he joined Tj after Grange accompanied Andrea to the shoot location.

"I think the ad is going to be great, and the fresh snow is an added bonus."

"Yeah, the storm was a pain, but I guess things worked out okay. Are you going to come with us to the ice-skating shoot?"

"Sure. I know I'm supposed to be helping though, and all I'm really doing is standing around. Do you need me to do anything specific?"

"Not really," Kyle said. "Arranging for the kids from the ski team to help out was huge, and Grange thought having someone on hand in case something did need to be done was a good idea."

"I'm here if you need me. Besides, it's good to focus on something other than Nolan's death and Stella's accident for a while."

"Is there any news about Stella?" Kyle asked.

"Not as of the last time I spoke to Hunter. She's stable and resting comfortably but still unconscious. I called Hunter again this morning, but he was dealing with an emergency and couldn't come to the phone. He hasn't called back yet, but I'll let you know when he does."

"Isn't it a little odd that Stella is breathing on her own and she still hasn't come to? Are they going to move her off the mountain?"

"I'm not sure," Tj answered. "Hunter wasn't sure what they were going to do the last time we spoke. I guess at some point they'll move her to a long-term care facility if she doesn't wake up, but Hunter seemed to think she would open her eyes and return to the living any day now. I hope he's right."

"Yeah. Me too."

"I do have some input on the on the Nolan front, that has provided a new perspective" Tj continued.

"Oh and what is that?"

"My dad suggested that the phone call to Murphy's might be a decoy."

Kyle frowned. "How so?"

"Dad pointed out that it would be incredibly stupid of the killer to use Nolan's phone to make a call to a public place and then put the phone back into Nolan's pocket where the cops were sure to find it. At first I wasn't too sure about the decoy angle but it does seem like we've spent a lot of time running down the intended recipient of the call that we could have used to investigate the possible murder."

"Your dad makes a good point. The killer would have to be pretty clueless to have done things the way we'd previously imagined he or she had. Should we ditch the call angle and work on something else?"

"Maybe. If we happen to have the opportunity to speak to someone who was at Murphy's that day, then we should but I wouldn't spend too much time on it."

"It' looks like I'm needed," Kyle commented as the camera man waved him over. "We'll talk some more later."

After they finished filming the downhill scenes the group headed into town to have lunch and then work on the ice-skating ones. As they had before, Oliver and Stephanie taped the action shots while Andrea and Brad looked on. The skating pond was on the lake at the edge of town, so hundreds of spectators had shown up to watch what many considered to be a once-in-a-lifetime event.

Tj watched Andrea as she interacted with her fans. Jenna had been correct when she'd said that Andrea was friendly and gracious to those who approached her. She greeted each person with a genuine smile, answered any questions that were asked, and signed what had to amount to hundreds of autographs. The woman was obviously good at what she did, and she worked the crowd better than anyone Tj had ever seen.

"I figured I'd find you in the middle of this." Hunter walked up behind Tj and kissed her on the cheek.

"It's quite the mob scene," Tj said. "I should have brought the girls. They would have enjoyed watching the ice skaters."

"Which is exactly what I thought, so I went to pick them up. Rosalie was at the house and promised to keep an eye on the puppies, so I brought Ben too." Hunter referred to Rosalie Taylor, the local veterinarian and her dad's girlfriend. "They're over there, near the benches, with Grandpa."

Tj looked across the pond to where Ben and Jake were sitting with Ashley and Gracie. "That was nice of you."

Hunter shrugged. "I figured they would enjoy it and I knew you'd be tied up. Besides, I knew both of our grandfathers could use a distraction. Nolan's death has been hard on them."

"Yeah," Tj agreed. "I haven't seen Grandpa this upset in a long time. Maybe not since Grandma died. I just can't imagine who would have done such a thing. The thought that whoever killed Nolan knew him well enough to be invited inside is almost too much to deal with."

"We don't know that for certain," Hunter pointed out.

"True. But based on what Grandpa overheard, it really seems that way."

"And Ben can't remember anything about the other voice?" Hunter asked.

"He says no. He heard Nolan open the door and greet whoever was on the other side, and then there was the sound of a struggle and the phone went dead. It could have been anyone."

"Maybe not *anyone*. Nolan was strong for his age, and he'd trained in self-defense. For a person to overpower him like that, he must have been strong. The killer also most likely knew exactly what he was doing. I haven't talked to either Tim or Roy; do they have any leads at all?" Hunter asked.

"Not really. They didn't find any fingerprints that seemed out of place, and the tracks through the woods were made by snowshoes. Large ones, so they think the person who made them was a large man. The tracks led out to the old service road, where snowmobile tracks led to the highway, but the plow had come through by the time they checked, so there were no tire tracks to identify. Like I said, whoever killed Nolan seemed to know what he was doing."

"And those are the only tracks that were found?"

"Yeah. He used the same path Nolan had used to get from the house to the shed in the first place and then again to get back to the house with Nolan's body. After he asphyxiated him, he returned along the same path between the house and the shed and then between the shed and the street where he left his car."

"Don't worry." Hunter squeezed her shoulder. "We'll get whoever did this."

"I hope so. Oh, wow, did you see that?" Tj clapped along with the rest of the crowd when Stephanie executed a perfect triple axel. If she wasn't such a fantastic skier Tj might encourage her to focus on her ice skating.

"She's really good. And Oliver is doing a good job of keeping up with her."

"Yeah, they make a good team. By the way, how is Stella today?" Tj asked.

"Actually, although she's still not awake, she's been moving around a bit. The night nurse reported that she moved both her hand and her leg while she was checking on her, and the daytime staff have confirmed similar movement this morning. I'm willing to say she's on her way back. There may even be more improvement by the end of the day. I am having her monitored very closely."

"That's wonderful," Tj said with relief. "I've been so worried about her. Please let me know if she comes to. I'll come right over. I'm sure she'll want to be assured that Kai and the puppies are okay. I took a bunch of photos of them playing with Echo and the girls to show her so she's assured that they're happy and fine."

"I just want to warn you that Stella may not remember everything right away when she wakes up. While it's possible she'll wake up and act like she's simply had a nap, it's equally possible that she'll be confused. She could even suffer a memory loss."

"Like amnesia?" Tj asked.

"Generalized amnesia is possible, but it's more likely that she'll suffer a short-term loss of specific details or a particular period of time. I'm not telling you this to scare you; I just want you to be prepared for whatever could occur when she comes to."

"I want to be there for her when she wakes up," Tj insisted. "If she's disoriented she might be scared."

"The nursing staff will call me the minute there's a change and I promise I'll call you."

"Thanks. I appreciate that. Are you off work for the rest of the day?"

"Unless something comes up. Do you want to do something when you're done here?"

"I wish I could, but I'm afraid they plan to film both a sledding and a snowmobiling scene after this."

"Maybe the grandpas, the girls, and I will tag along, if that's okay."

"I'd like that." Tj smiled. "I was thinking that—"

"Coach Jensen, Dr. Hanson," one of the other members of her ski team interrupted.

"Hi, Joy. What can I do for you?" Tj asked.

"I'm sorry to interrupt, but Stephanie said you might need some additional skaters in the background. I brought my skates." Joy held up a pair of white skates.

"See that man over there in the blue sweater standing next to Kyle?" Tj pointed to the director. "His name is Grange. He's in charge of the shoot, so you might want to ask him."

"Thanks. I will. Oh, and is downhill practice back on for Monday?"

"It is as long as the wind doesn't kick back up. Check your email on Sunday evening. I should know for sure by then."

"Okay, thanks again. I'll see you in class."

Tj watched as Joy trotted over to where a group of her friends, all with their own skates, waited. She said something to Kyle, who spoke to Grange, who must have been fine with the idea because the girls squealed loud enough to be heard from where she was standing.

"You were thinking that...?" Hunter prompted.

Tj stared at him blankly.

"Before Joy came over you were about to say something."

"Oh, yeah. I was thinking maybe we could do something tomorrow evening, if you're off. Jenna and I are taking the four girls to lunch to try to patch things up between Ashley and Kristi, but I should be free by midday. It seems like it's been forever since we've spent any quality time together."

"I'd like that very much. Maybe dinner at my place? I know our grandpas and some of the others from the senior center are planning to get together tomorrow evening to play some poker and talk about Nolan. I'm dropping him off at five, and he said he'll need to be picked up at ten, but I'm free in between."

"If Dad can watch the girls you have a date. I'll drop my grandpa off at the senior center on my way over and then I can just pick him up on the way home."

"Chinese or pizza?" Hunter asked.

"Let's pick up Chinese. Jenna and I are taking the girls to Rob's for lunch."

"Chinese it is. It looks like Kyle is waving you over."

Tj grabbed Hunter's hand. "Come with me. Maybe you can help."

After the ice-skating shots had been completed, the entire entourage packed up and headed toward the sledding hill. Grange wanted a lot of kids sledding down the hill in the background, so he allowed those spectators with sleds to have at it within the boundaries he outlined.

While they had begun the day as a small group, they'd picked up hundreds of spectators as the day wore on. Filming an ad, especially one starring Andrea Washburn, was the biggest thing to happen in the small town of Serenity in a very long time.

"Looks like the young ones are having a good time." Jake Hanson rolled his wheelchair over to where Tj was standing as they watched the sledding from the parking lot. Hunter had taken the girls to the sledding hill and Ben was speaking to Frannie Edison, the town librarian.

"It really does. I'd join them myself, but I'm supposed to be helping. The thing is, so far all I've done is stand around and watch."

Jake chuckled. "You do it well. So, Hunter tells me you're taking me to my physical therapy on Monday."

"I am," Tj confirmed.

"Guess he figures you can get me to do my exercises."

"He does."

"I'm an old man who was practicing medicine before your father was born. I know what needs to be done, and as much as I appreciate your willingness to trouble yourself, I don't need a nursemaid to keep an eye on me," Jake stubbornly pointed out.

Tj turned to look Jake in the eye. "If you know what needs to be done, why aren't you doing it?"

"I'm doing it," Jake defended himself.

Tj lifted one eyebrow, continuing to look him in the eye.

"Most of the time," Jake countered.

"Hunter loves you. I love you," Tj emphasized. "We want you to be as healthy as you can possibly be."

"Let's face it," Jake groaned, "I don't have lot of years left. From where I'm sitting, it doesn't seem worth the bother."

"Poppycock. You've had a physical setback. A serious one. You're used to being the doctor and not the patient. It doesn't sit well to have people fussing over you, telling you what to do and when to do it. It's not easy to ask for and accept help from others. I get that. I'm sorry this is hard for you. I really am. But feeling sorry for yourself isn't going to get you to the place you need to be. Don't you want to walk again?"

"Of course I want to walk," Jake snapped. Tj could see Jake was getting mad. That was good; Tj could deal with mad.

"Then make the commitment to get up out of that chair. The physical therapist told Hunter that with the right exercise you can walk again. You just need to follow the program."

"Easy for you to say. You're young. You're healthy. Your whole life is ahead of you, while I'm looking in the rearview mirror at mine."

"You're scared," Tj realized.

"Of course I'm scared. I'm not ready to move on from my time on this earth. There's still so much I'm waiting for."

"Like what?" Tj asked gently.

"For one thing, I always figured I'd be around to meet my great-grandchildren. Chelsea has no interest in marriage or children, and at the rate you and Hunter are taking things, Methuselah wouldn't have lived long enough to enjoy the fruit of your love."

Tj placed her hand over Jake's and gave it a gentle squeeze. "I can't promise you that Hunter and I will get married, and I can't promise you that even if we did we'd have children right away. But we're working on our relationship, and if you promise me to do everything your physical therapist tells you, I promise to consider my timeline from your perspective."

"So you think the two of you might get hitched?" Jake grinned.

"I didn't say that," Tj backpedaled. Hunter was going to

kill her. "I just said I'll keep your desire to meet your great-grandchildren in mind. I realize our current status is stalled at best. I guess I didn't see the hurry to figure things out, and you know Hunter and I can't get married just to give you great-grandchildren. Still, I should take the time I need to commit or not to the relationship. If I don't think there's a future for us, I should be honest with Hunter so he can move on, and if I do think we have a future, maybe it's time to take the next step."

"Sounds reasonable," Jake agreed.

"So can I come with you on Monday?" Tj asked.

"Yeah. You can come."

CHAPTER 8

When Tj had finished helping Kyle she headed over to the sheriff's office to speak to Roy and Tim while Hunter took the grandpas and the girls for ice cream sundaes. She hoped they'd made some progress in the murder case. Roy and Tim were both good cops, and Tj knew she should just leave the investigation to them, but there was a part of her that knew she'd never fully relax until the person who'd killed a wonderful man like Nolan was brought to justice.

Tj decided to walk the short distance between the ice cream shop and the sheriff's office. The sun was out, the temperature almost tepid, and the sky bluer than she could remember seeing it in a long while. The businesses along Main Street were all open and the streets had been cleared of all traces of the snow that had fallen the previous week, allowing visitors to come up the mountain for a weekend of skiing and snowboarding.

The Serenity branch of the Paradise County Sheriff's Department was no more than a small brick building tucked behind the county offices. Being a satellite office, it contained a single holding cell, which was utilized only until a suspect in custody could be transported to the larger jail in

Indulgence for booking and lockup. The reception area was little more than a tiny square room with an L-shaped counter, behind which was a desk with a handheld radio and a wall of file cabinets. Small windows placed high on the wall let a modest amount of light into the otherwise drab room.

"Thought you were helping with the commercial," Tim commented when Tj walked through the front door, stomping the snow from her boots.

"I was, but they're moving on to the indoor scenes, so they really didn't need me. I wanted to stop by while I had a few minutes to talk about the investigation. Is Roy around?"

"He's off tonight, but it's slow right now so I can chat. Have a seat."

Tj sat down on an armless chair that was positioned in front of the desk that was shared by everyone who covered the front office. Currently, there were three employees working in the Serenity office: Roy Fisher, the senior deputy, Tim Matthews, his assistant, and a front-office clerk.

"So do you have any news or new leads since the last time we spoke?" Tj asked as she tried to ignore the jelly stain on Tim's shirt.

"Not really. Roy pulled the original file from the fire that killed that young couple," Tim informed her. "The name of the arresting officer was blacked out on every document, and several documents that should be there are missing altogether. It's been fifteen years, so we are having a hard time finding out who might have tampered with the paperwork. The sheriff in charge at the time is deceased and the clerk who worked in the records department has long since retired and moved from the area."

"Figures." Tj sighed.

"I did manage to have a chat with Jerry Johnson."

Tj remembered Jerry Johnson was one of the four deputies to initially respond to the fire.

"He said he was on shift on the south shore the day Nolan was killed and I verified that with dispatch. In fact, dispatch confirmed that both Johnson and Boggs were on shift on the south shore the entire week of the blizzard so I guess you can take them off your list."

"So you have nothing." Tj groaned in frustration.

"I didn't say that," Tim answered. "I did find a couple of things that seem interesting."

"Such as?" Tj probed.

"For one thing, I found copies of the fire marshal's report for both fires. Unfortunately, they mean nothing to me. I really need to have someone from the fire department look at them, but with the snow and then the extra security needed as a result of the commercial, we've been stretched pretty thin."

"I'll take them and ask Dennis to look at them," Tj volunteered.

Tim hesitated.

"I know that allowing me to have copies of the documents is against procedure, and Boggs would have a coronary if he found out, but he won't find out," Tj promised. "Dennis is home and I'm free at the moment, so let me play courier."

"I could just call Dennis and ask him to come in," Tim pointed out.

"He's watching the girls while Jenna's at work. You know me; I've helped you before. Let me go talk to Dennis, and then I'll come back to tell you everything he said."

"I guess that would be the most efficient way to handle things." Tim got up and walked across the room to the copy machine.

"Did you find anything else?" Tj asked.

"I found additional correspondence from the district attorney. It's clear to me that they planned to cut Clay Warner loose due to errors made during the arrest even before the second fire. If you ask me, the second fire was a smoke screen to cover up the real reason the man was released from custody."

"Yeah, that's what Kyle and I thought as well. I'd bet a month's wages that the second fire was set by someone in law enforcement at the time of the error that might have ended one or more careers if it had been made public."

Tim handed Tj the copies of the reports.

"Anything else?" Tj asked.

"No, that's it."

"Okay thanks. I'll call you or come back by after I talk to Dennis." Tj turned to leave when Roy walked in through the door behind her. "I thought you were off."

"I am. I just came back for a file I forgot."

"Tim was just filling me in on the initial fire reports for the two fires surrounding the Clay Warren case."

"She is going to ask Dennis to look at them," Tim informed Roy, who was both his friend and his superior. "I didn't think you'd mind."

"I don't mind. Dennis is the logical person to help us out." Roy turned and looked at Tj. "Actually I'm glad I ran into you. I chatted with the records clerk for a few minutes when I called the main office looking for the original copies of Warner's arrest, and she informed me—off the record, of course—that Nolan had been in requesting copies of three case files. One was the fire, which we know about, the second was the extra body in the coffin, and the third was a discharge of firearms arrest involving a minor."

"What minor?" Tj asked.

"The juvenile file has been sealed and the clerk either didn't know or wouldn't say. Here's the interesting thing about the third arrest: the gun used in the discharge of firearms case was a service weapon that supposedly had been assigned to the armory."

Tj remembered that Nolan had been at the shooting range the day before the storm hit, and the armory was located on the property. Maybe Hazel hadn't been all that far off the mark when she asserted that Nolan had been investigating that day, which had turned out to be the last time anyone had seen him alive.

"Walk me through the significance of that," Tj said.

"All the weapons owned by the county are registered through a system that's designed to keep track of the physical location of every individual piece. Some weapons are assigned to personnel and others are kept in the armory. The weapons in the armory are used mainly for target practice and training at the shooting range, which is important for employees trying to earn certification on a specific weapon. It allows them to check a weapon out for training purposes, practice, and then turn it back in at the end of the day."

"Okay, so who was the weapon checked out to in this case?" Tj asked.

"No one. According to the database, the gun should have been in the armory. No one even knew it was missing."

"So someone stole it?" Tj guessed.

"Either that or the officer in charge of the armory turned a blind eye as the gun walked away. The whole thing makes no sense, really," Roy commented. "Why steal a gun and then give it to your kid to use for target practice?"

"Yeah, something isn't adding up," Tj agreed. "Do you think the fire and subsequent botched arrest, extra body in the coffin, and illegal discharge of firearms incident are all related?"

"Honestly, I have no idea. For all I know, Nolan was looking into three distinct cases that weren't then and aren't now in any way related to one another."

"I doubt the missing gun has anything to do with Nolan's death," Tim added. "Those guns turn up missing more often than anyone would want to admit. The county likes to give the impression that they have a secure system but they really don't. My money is on the internal cover-up at the time of Clay Warren's release."

"You're probably right. I did think the extra body in the coffin could be relevant but I'm hitting a dead end there. It seems the only employee who is still around from the time when the extra body would have been placed in the coffin is the grounds keeper and I haven't managed to track him down."

"What do you mean at the time the body was placed in the coffin?" Roy asked. "How do we know when that was?"

Tj explained that Kyle had found out about the two-day lag time between the funeral and the burial due to the storm and his theory that the body was added at that time. "If that is true then it seems that the person who put the body in the coffin must have had an accomplice at the funeral home."

"Why would anyone from the funeral home help a killer

dispose of a body?" Tim asked. "The Serenity Funeral Home was family owned and operated back then. I don't see anyone helping a killer to cover up evidence. Still I don't suppose it would hurt to talk to the groundskeeper."

"I'll stop by on my way home," Roy answered.

"No way," Tim countered. "It is your day off. If you end up working on your day off, you'll expect me to work on my day off and I have plans with a special lady."

Roy shrugged. "Suit yourself but it sounds like Kyle has a logical theory so someone should follow up."

"I'll do it," Tj offered.

"You were going to talk to Dennis about the reports from the two fires," Tim reminded her. "I'll do it and then we'll meet back up and compare notes."

"Okay. It's probably a good idea you talk to him anyway. You might have more success. I don't know the guy so there's no reason he'd talk to me. I'll head over to talk to Dennis and then I'll be back." Tj stood up.

"Okay the two of you seem to have it handled so I'll head home," Roy stated. "Do call me if either of you come up with something relevant. I want to get this case solved day off or not."

Tj headed back to the ice cream parlor, where she'd left Hunter with the grandpas and the girls. She explained that she needed a little more time, so he offered to take the group to a movie and then meet up with her later. It looked like everyone in the group was having a lot of fun, so Tj agreed to the plan and then headed over to the house on the river that Dennis, Jenna, and their girls shared.

"What brings you to the insane asylum?" Dennis asked when he answered the door.

"Girls still going bonkers?"

"Bonkers would be how I would have described them two days ago. Now I'd say they've graduated to manic, but they're both feeling better, and Jenna tells me the two of you will be taking them to what I hope will be a very long lunch tomorrow. The thought of sitting in a silent house with only the basketball game for company sounds like heaven."

Dennis closed the door behind her as Tj walked in and hung up her coat. She could hear the girls laughing and screaming from upstairs. "I hoped you could look at these incident reports with me. They're from the fires Nolan was looking into when he died."

"Be happy to. Let's sit at the kitchen table. It's a little farther away from the circus going on upstairs."

Tj followed Dennis into the kitchen. She sat down at the dark oak table while he poured them each a cup of coffee. Jenna really was lucky to have Dennis. He was kind and patient, as well as tall, strong, and a total babe. And best of all, he loved Jenna and his crazy girls with all his heart.

Dennis sat down across from Tj and opened the folder to access the files Roy had copied. "Am I looking for anything specific?" he asked.

"I don't know. Nolan seemed to think there was something odd about the case, but other than the fact that the arresting officer apparently botched the arrest, we really don't know why he was looking into the case. I figured if you looked at the files something might pop."

Dennis had been hired on by the local fire department as a trainee the day after he graduated high school. He was good at his job and knew more about fires and fire patterns than most.

"It looks like the fires were set in a similar way. The structure was doused with gasoline and then a device with a crude timer was set. In the incident of the cabin, a long fuse was attached to a small explosive device."

"A small explosive device?" Tj asked.

"Something like a cherry bomb. My guess is that whoever burned down the cabin set the device near the center of the structure and then doused the surrounding area with the gasoline. The cabin from the first fire was an old building made of wood. It would have gone up in flames in minutes. If I had to guess, the path along which the fuse was laid hadn't been doused with gasoline, which allowed the fuse to burn all the way to the end."

"How long would it take for the flame to connect with the device once set?" Tj asked.

"It depends on the length of the fuse, but not long. Probably minutes, if that."

"So the arsonist was still in the area when the cabin went up in flames?"

"Most likely. If I remember the case correctly, the person who set the fire tied up the young couple who lived there and then set the fire. It seems obvious that the incident was more about killing the couple in some sort of ceremonial way than it was about the arson."

"What do you mean?" Tj asked.

"If someone simply wanted to kill these poor people, there were certainly easier ways to go about it. No, the person who did this wanted to make a statement."

Which led back to Clay Warner, Tj realized, who most likely was guilty, only someone had screwed up and the man had been set free.

"Is there anything that stands out as different between the two fires?" Tj asked.

Dennis studied the reports. "The fuse in the first fire was crude and obviously handmade, while the one used in the second was a high-quality product, most likely purchased from a supplier."

Tj frowned. "I thought the fires were supposed to have been identical."

"They are similar, and I can see how someone without special training might come to the conclusion that they were set by the same person. But I've taken special courses in investigation since I hope to be promoted to captain one day, and from a trained eye they don't look all that identical."

"What are the major differences?"

"Like I said, the major difference is material used. It looks like the first fire was set by someone who rounded up a bunch of stuff he or she found on hand to do the deed, while the second seemed to have been set by someone who knew what he or she wanted to accomplish beforehand and gathered the necessary materials."

"So maybe Clay Warner didn't go to the cabin with the intention of burning it down. Maybe he went there to reason with the couple, to try to talk them into giving him his home back. When they refused, he snapped, tied them up, looked around the property, where he found the gasoline and the other materials he needed, and then set the fire to send a message," Tj formulated.

"It looks like everything that was used in the first fire was stuff you'd have on hand," Dennis agreed.

"Would it be reasonable that someone like Clay would know how to build a cherry bomb?"

"Sure. Cherry bombs are easy to build and the information on how to build them is readily available. My friends and I used to build small ones all the time just to watch them explode."

"Thanks, Dennis. I'm not sure this helps us with Nolan's death, but it does seem to confirm my suspicion that the second fire was set to cover up the mistake made by the arresting deputy. Now if we can just find out who that was, we might have a solid suspect."

Tj chatted with Dennis for a few minutes before she left and went back to the sheriff's office to fill Tim in on their conversation. Tim assured her that he'd fill Roy in and then reported that he'd spoken to the grounds keeper who verified that the body had been buried two days after the funeral. He dug the grave but was not personally responsible for transporting the body to the cemetery or setting the coffin in the grave. He informed Tim that the previous owners of the funeral home were good folk who cared about the community and he very much doubted that the body had been added to the coffin at this point. He also testified that he didn't remember anyone acting suspiciously at the time of the burial.

Tj then headed over to the movie theater to meet up with Hunter, the grandpas, and the girls. The sun had set while she was talking to Dennis, reminding her that it was about time to start thinking about dinner. Maybe she'd take Ben and the girls out for a bite before heading back to the resort, unless her grandfather was exhausted from his day in town and ready to head home directly.

Tj pulled up in front of the theater a good fifteen minutes before the end of the movie, just in time to see Hunter running from the entrance.

"Oh, good, you're here," Hunter said as he jogged up to her car.

"I just got here. What's up?"

"I just got a text from the hospital. Stella is awake. I have to go. Can you take everyone home?"

"Absolutely. Can I see her?"

Hunter took a deep breath. "I don't know. Let me see exactly what's going on and then I'll call you." Hunter kissed her on the lips and then took off running toward the parking lot and his car.

CHAPTER 9

Sunday, March 15

"Welcome back sleepy head," Tj smiled at Stella after Hunter cleared her for a visit.

"Tj I'm so glad to see you. How is Kai?"

"Kai is fine. She misses you but my sister Gracie is taking good care of her and the puppies, and Echo is really in his element playing uncle for a few days. See, I brought photos."

Stella sighed as she looked at the photos on my phone. "I'm glad Kai and the babies are doing well and aren't proving to be too much trouble. Puppies can be a real handful at this age."

"They've been no trouble at all," Tj lied.

"I can't believe that I've been in here for so long. I feel like I've simply waken from a nap."

Tj sat down on the edge of the bed, "I'll admit that you had us scared for a while. I'm happy that you are back with us. How do you feel?'"

"Tired which is ridiculous since I've just had the longest nap of my life, and a little achy."

"Do you remember what happened?"

"Not all of it. I remember it was snowing and I was taking it slow and then all of the sudden there were headlights coming straight toward me. The next thing I knew I woke up here hungrier than I've ever been in my life."

"I hope the nursing staff fed you."

"They did. They've all been so nice but I really want to go home. Unfortunately, I'm being told I need to stay for a few more days. They want to do additional testing to make sure my brain isn't scrambled."

"I know you are anxious to get back to your life but you suffered a serious injury. I think a few more days is a good idea."

"Can you do me a favor?"

"Anything."

"Can you go by my house and set up my DVR to record my favorite shows. I'm going to be so lost if I miss any more episodes."

Tj laughed. "I'd be happy to. What shows do you want me to record?"

"I'll make you a list. Oh can you grab Kai's vitamins. Nursing mom's need extra nutrients. And you'll need to water my plants. And check on my neighbor. She doesn't drive and depends on me to get to the pharmacy and grocery store. I'll make you a list."

"Don't worry," Tj assured her. "I'll take care of everything."

"So far so good." Tj slowly let out the breath she'd been holding since she'd shown up at Rob's Pizza with Ashley and

Gracie in tow. During the first tense minutes Kristi and Ashley had avoided eye contact, but once Gracie suggested playing video games the tension had been broken and furtive glances were replaced by squeals of joy.

"I had a long talk with Kristi, and she's agreed to let it go and not bring it up as long as Ashley stops gossiping about her," Jenna informed Tj as she watched Ashley and Kristi high-five each other over an apparent video-game victory.

"And I had a long talk with Ashley, who is very sorry for what she said and promises not to repeat it," Tj said. "She agreed to apologize to Kristi, but I'm not sure she ever will. I was going to insist on it, but it seems like they've moved past this whole mess on their own and I don't want to jinx it."

"Yeah, they seem to be having fun. I'd leave it alone. I've never been a fan of the forced apology anyway. It's usually pretty obvious that the person giving it is doing so under duress and doesn't really mean it. How'd the shoot go yesterday?" Jenna asked.

"Really good." Tj turned away from the activity in the game room and looked at Jenna. "It was a beautiful day, the actors were super nice, and Andrea stopped to chat with everyone who came out to watch. I know they got some awesome shots. The commercial is going to be fantastic."

"I'm really glad," Jenna said. "I wanted to come out to watch myself, but we were slammed. It seems like now that the snow has stopped half the people in the valley have driven up the mountain to play in the white stuff. I'm glad we're closed on Sundays. I think there are as many people in town today as there were yesterday."

"Everyone has ski fever with all the fresh powder," Tj agreed. "I'd love to be on the mountain myself, but this was more important. Besides, the ski team and I will be on the mountain preparing for the regional competition tomorrow, so I can get my powder time in then. It's too bad Andrea doesn't ski. She would be in heaven with the perfect conditions."

"Andrea doesn't ski?" Jenna asked.

"Apparently not. I had a couple of students volunteer to do the action shots while Brad and Andrea provided the close-ups."

"I guess I just assumed she would ski because I'd heard she used to live here," Jenna commented.

"She said she only lived in the area for a few years. I don't remember her at all, though I know she went to Serenity High. I think she's at least a few years older than us."

"Rob was three years ahead of us in high school. We should ask him if he remembers her when he comes over to take our order," Jenna suggested.

"Speak of the devil." Tj grinned when Rob walked up with his notepad.

"Now I'm the devil?" Rob asked. "What'd I do?"

"Nothing. We were just wondering, do you remember Andrea Washburn from high school?" Tj asked.

"She went to Serenity High?" Rob asked.

"So she said," Tj answered.

Rob stopped to think about it. "The name isn't ringing a bell, but I have all my yearbooks in the back. I'll grab them and we can look her up."

"You keep your high school yearbook in the kitchen of your place of business?" Jenna asked.

"Sometimes people from the old days come in, and even

though I recognize them I can't remember their names, so I look them up, and when I go over to take their order I can pretend I never forgot them."

"That's actually a really good idea," Jenna complimented. "I've had the same thing happen at the Antiquery. Someone will come in and I'll recognize their face but can't quite match it with a name. When that happens I pray it will come to me as I'm desperately trying to figure out a way to get the person to mention their name during the conversation. I can't tell you how many times I've greeted old classmates with 'hey you.'"

Rob laughed. "Why don't you go ahead and give me your order? I'll drop it off in the kitchen when I go back to grab the books."

Tj and Jenna ordered two large pizzas, one cheese for the kids and the other with the works for them. Rob's pizza was thick and cheesy, and his sauce was better than any Tj had ever eaten. Her stomach rumbled while she waited for the salads she and Jenna had ordered as well.

Tj sipped her soda as she once again glanced into the game room. She could hear squeals of victory as the four girls mastered the electronic devices that almost overpowered the room with their bells and whistles. She was so grateful that Kristi was so mature and well-adjusted. If not for her, and the leadership she provided, poor Ashley wouldn't have any friends at all.

By the time Rob returned with the yearbooks a waitress had brought Tj and Jenna their salads and they had begun to nibble on the fresh greens.

"Here we go." Rob slid into the booth next to Tj. Rob, Tj, and Jenna each looked through a different book, the individual class photos were listed alphabetically, so they turned to the back.

"I found her," Rob announced, pointing to the photo of a super-thin girl with white skin and long black hair after a few minutes.

"Andrea Washburn is a blonde," Jenna pointed out.

"Maybe she dyed her hair when she was in high school," Rob suggested. "Everyone used to call her Goth girl. She had that long black hair and always wore black clothes and tons of black makeup."

Tj looked at the girl's black eyeliner and black lipstick.

"She had this whole moody thing going on. She never smiled or spoke to anyone other than those in her Goth group."

"Goth group?" Jenna asked. "There were others?"

"Yeah. Quite a few, actually. It was a huge fad when I was in high school."

"I remember hearing about the fad on television, but I don't remember it being a really big thing at Paradise Lake," Jenna said.

"It only lasted a couple of years up here, but it was a real thing for a while," Rob explained.

"Who else was in this Goth group?" Tj asked.

"Brandon Halliwell, for one," Rob answered as he flipped through the book.

"Brandon?" Tj had to admit she was shocked. If anything, Tj would classify Brandon as a redneck. He wore fatigues around town, he owned a guns and ammo store, and he took his weapons seriously. He had guns for hunting and others for target practice, while the handgun in his drawer at the store was known to everyone as the Warden.

"Back in high school Brandon had a thing for Andrea. It seemed to the rest of us like he was just doing the dark knight thing to impress Andrea. Once she left town he traded his black garb for the hunting clothes he's been wearing ever since."

Rob found Brandon's picture. Sure enough, Brandon Halliwell had dyed his hair jet black and wore the same dark eyeliner as Andrea.

"I bet his dad had a coronary the first time Brandon showed up looking like that." Tj laughed.

"Tell me about it," Jenna agreed. "I would never have guessed that Brandon had ever been anything but a gun-toting hillbilly. He looks so different. I would never have recognized him if I had seen this photo out of context."

"How about you?" Tj asked Rob. "What high school clique were you most identified with?"

"Me? I was king of the nerds."

Tj laughed. "You aren't a nerd. In fact, you're one of the most popular guys in town."

"That was before my growth spurt, before I traded my glasses for contacts and my braces came off. In high school—nerd. Look, here I am." Rob turned to a photo of a skinny kid with long hair, thick glasses, and wires covering all his teeth.

"Yikes."

"Yikes is right. It turned out okay though. I guess I was just a late bloomer. How about you, Miss Head Cheerleader?" Rob turned to Tj. "Any secret cliques you popular girls identified with, or were the rest of us too far beneath you even to consider?"

Tj thought about it. "I can't remember longing to be in any particular group, and while I'll admit I was popular, that might have had more to do with the fact that I was dating Hunter Hanson than anything else. And I wasn't *only* a cheerleader. I had depth. I was on the honor roll all four years, and I joined both the ski and track teams. I also played softball in the summer," Tj added.

"I was just teasing you." Rob stood up. "I need to get back to work, but feel free to look through the yearbook. I'll stop back by to get it when your pizzas are done."

Tj and Jenna continued to look through the books page by page. It was fun to see how those members of the community who were a few years older than them looked when they were teenagers.

"Oh, wow, check out Brian Strongman." Tj laughed. The boy in the picture was tall and thin, with a full head of hair that hung down his back. He now owned the local dry cleaner's and was bald and portly a mere fifteen years later. "Time hasn't been kind to poor Brian."

"On the other hand, check out Beverly Newman." Jenna pointed to a photo. The girl had glasses, braces, and acne, but Tj knew she had gone on to become one of the most beautiful women in town. "Or Tim Matthews," Jenna added.

"Wow, look at the long hair. He's really different now. I don't think I looked all that much different in high school than I do now," Tj commented.

"This makes me want to go home and dig out our old yearbooks," Jenna told her. "Remember that photo of you and Hunter and Dennis and me at the prom? We were going through the big hair phase, and both Hunter and Dennis had long hair past their collars. I really need to find it."

"We had a lot of fun, didn't we?" Tj asked nostalgically. "The four of us were a good team." Tj and Hunter had dated all through high school. Tj thought they'd grow old together until Hunter gave into pressure from his mother and ended their love affair during their junior year of college. In some ways Tj didn't really blame Hunter for what had occurred. They'd been young, and he had big shoes to fill. They'd tried to make a go of it but in the end their love hadn't been strong enough to weather the challenges being a Hanson heir provided.

"Yeah, we did have a lot of fun," Jenna agreed. "And we still do. All this looking back has suddenly made me feel old. The four of us should go out and do something next weekend. We can get wild and crazy, and maybe even stay out until ten." She laughed.

"Sounds like fun," Tj agreed. "Hunter and I are having dinner tonight. I'll ask him."

"Let's do it on Saturday night," Jenna suggested. "That way I won't have to get up early to go to work."

"Yeah, Saturday will be better for me as well, and Hunter usually has weekends off unless there's an emergency."

"Speaking of emergencies, did you get in to see Stella this morning?"

"I did," Tj confirmed.

"And how is she?"

"She seems fine. It's so odd. The memory of the accident itself is fuzzy to her, but other than that it's like she just took a long nap. She was shocked to find out that she'd been unconscious for almost a week."

"That would be strange," Jenna agreed.

"She's so funny." Tj smiled. "The first thing she did when she saw me was ask about Kai and the puppies, but once I reassured her that they were fine and showed her the photos

I'd taken, she asked me to go to her house to check her DVR. She wanted to be sure all her shows were recording correctly."

Jenna laughed. "It's funny the things we put a priority on. When will she be able to go home?"

"Hunter wasn't sure. They're going to keep her a few more days at least so they can do some additional testing. If all goes well she might be out by midweek. Gracie is going to be crushed when those puppies go home, but to be honest, I'll be glad to see them go."

"What? The dog lady isn't thrilled with having three puppies running around the house?" Jenna teased.

"Don't get me wrong: I love Echo and I love Kai and the puppies, but with everything that's been going on I haven't had the time to monitor the little rugrats the way I should. I think the dogs have teamed up to take over the house, and in spite of my efforts to maintain order, they seem to be winning."

Jenna chuckled.

"Not only have the puppies peed on every surface they've managed to gain access to but one of them decided that Grandpa's new slippers were chew toys. It wasn't pleasant when he discovered the slobbery mess."

"Oh, no. Don't you have a pen?"

"I set up a space in one of the spare rooms, but Gracie keeps sneaking them out. I've talked to her, Dad has talked to her, and Grandpa has made it clear that the puppies aren't allowed downstairs, but she insists on sneaking them down anyway. I suppose I should punish her, but then she makes a comment about them being sad because they're missing Stella and I get all gooey inside."

"The girl has got your number for sure."

"Yeah." Tj sighed. "I guess she does. I'm really looking forward to my child-free date with Hunter tonight."

"So where are you two going?"

"His place. Jake and Grandpa and a few of their friends are getting together to play cards and talk about their feelings about Nolan's murder, so Hunter and I are going to drop our respective grandfathers off at the senior center and pick up some takeout."

"Sounds relaxing. And intimate." Jenna grinned.

"We're just friends," Tj automatically replied. *We're just friends* had been her automatic response for so long that she said it without thinking, but even she had to wonder if that was still true.

Tj thought about her conversation with Jake earlier in the day. Hunter seemed to want to try, and deep in her heart, Tj knew that if the choice was limited to going all in or walking away, she'd be all in in a heartbeat. It had been safe playing the just-friends game, but Jake wasn't wrong about the fact that Hunter deserved to have a family, whether it was with her or someone else.

Tj looked directly at Jenna.

"Actually, I've been thinking about that. The friend thing," she clarified. "I think it's time for me to decide if Hunter and I can have a future."

"I agree," Jenna answered, "but you've been pretty adamant about wanting to keep things casual. What's changed?"

Tj replayed her conversation with Jake.

Jenna frowned. "While I think that figuring out where you and Hunter stand is a good idea, and while I'm on Team

Hunter all the way, I don't want to see you marry the guy just to make Jake happy. Marriage is a huge commitment that's hard and messy and at times makes you want to scream at the top of your lungs. It should never be entered into lightly."

Dennis and Jenna had been high school sweethearts who'd married right after they graduated and bought the house on the river with money both sets of parents had gifted them. They'd had Kristi a year later and Kari three years after that.

"Wow, way to sell wedded bliss."

Jenna smiled. "I love Dennis. I love being married to him. He's my best friend and soul mate and I wake up every morning thanking God that I have him in my life. But in spite of how wonderful and fulfilling being married to Dennis is, it's also a lot of hard work and compromise. He can be so clueless sometimes, and I can be a total nag when I'm stressed and tired. If we didn't *really* love each other, if we hadn't made a *real* commitment years ago, we would have killed each other by now."

"I get your point. And don't worry, I'm not going to marry Hunter just to make Jake happy. On the other hand, Jake's comment made me realize that I haven't really been fair to either Hunter or myself by insisting on this arm's length dating pattern that we've settled into. Either I love Hunter and want to work on building a life with him or I don't. I need to decide."

Jenna wound her hand through Tj's and gave it a gentle squeeze.

"If you decide to take the next step with Hunter be sure that you're able to accept the total package," she counseled. "The parts of him you love, the parts of him that irritate the crap out of you, and the part of him that broke your heart ten years ago. I love you and I love Hunter and I think you're great together, but marriage is definitely a whole package deal."

"Thanks," Tj said. "I'll keep that in mind."

CHAPTER 10

Monday, March 16

If the disaster that greeted Tj when she walked into her office upon returning to work was any indication of how the rest of the day was going to go, she thought she might as well go home, climb into her bed, and pull the covers over her head for the duration of the winter.

"What you mean, the plumber is tied up and can't get here for a couple more hours?" Tj complained. "There's a steady stream of water pouring down from the ceiling and a good foot of water already on the floor. I'm sure the files in the bottom drawers of the cabinet are already destroyed."

Not only had the heater gone out during the week the high school was closed, causing the pipes to freeze, but no one had realized that several of the pipes had cracked, sending a steady stream of water into the physical education offices, which were located in the basement of the new gym that had been built over the summer.

"I can assure you that the plumber promised to get here as soon as humanly possible," Greg Remington, the school principal, told her. "In the meantime we're going to close this entire building. You'll need to hold your classes in the cafeteria until the repairs can be made."

"How am I supposed to hold PE classes in the cafeteria? There's barely enough room to walk between the tables, let alone do any sort of activity." Tj knew she was being difficult, but her shoes were soaking wet, her jeans clung to her legs, and she suspected the something squishy she'd stepped on beneath the surface of the waterline wasn't mud.

Greg let out a long breath. "I don't know, Tj. Improvise. You aren't the only one who's being inconvenienced here. The boys' locker room is even a bigger mess than your office, and the very expensive flooring we just installed in the gym is surely ruined. I can guarantee you that I'm going to have to answer to the school finance committee for that one."

Tj closed her eyes and tried to mentally recite a mantra she often used during tense situations. *Deep breath in, filling my body with peace and serenity, long hold to settle into the calm, slow breath out, releasing all my stress and tension.* It wasn't working. She opened her eyes and looked around her office. Everything was ruined. One of the tiles in the ceiling overhead gave way, sending a river of water over her head. She was sure she was going to cry.

Principal Remington tried not to laugh as Tj wiped wet hair out of her face.

"It's not funny," Tj snapped.

"It's kind of funny." Greg chuckled.

Tj looked down at the thin shirt that clung to her chest. She looked like a kid on spring break trying to win a wet t-shirt contest. She was going to need to find something to change into before her first class.

"I'm really sorry," Greg tried again, "but there really isn't anything I can do. I need to get over to the office to see if I can get someone in here to dry this place out once the plumber gets the leaks fixed."

"Okay, I'll figure something out." Tj picked up her brand new fitness monitor, which she had spent a whole week's pay on, after Greg left. It was more than just a heart monitor. It was a computerized personal trainer that provided feedback of heart rate, oxygen intake, blood pressure, calories burned, and a dozen other things. She could tell from a single glance it was beyond saving. She tossed it aside as she noticed the soggy mass of paper that used to be the first edition of her favorite childhood book, which her dad had bought her when she was promoted to head of the department. Could this day get any worse?

Tj sat down on her wet desk chair and gave into the tears that had been threatening ever since she'd first arrived. Maybe she would have been able to deal with all of this better if she'd gotten any sleep the previous night. She had tried to sleep, but all she'd managed was to toss and turn as she psychoanalyzed her terrible date with Hunter. It hadn't been Hunter's fault. After her conversation with Jenna she'd found herself studying Hunter's every move almost actively, looking for that one annoying behavior that would prove to be a deal breaker. Poor Hunter thought they were just having one of their usual get-together, share-some-food, and watch-a-movie nights, but Tj knew it was so much more.

He'd noticed her weirdness and asked about it, but she'd just told him she was tired. She knew he didn't buy her explanation, but he'd graciously accepted it and seemed to go out of his way to make sure she was having a good time in spite of her grumpy mood. This, of course, led Tj to identify the first of what she was sure would prove to be a whole list of annoying habits: his tendency to try *way* too hard to make her happy.

Realizing she only had twenty minutes until her first class, Tj headed to the storage room, where extra physical education clothes were kept. Each student was assigned one pair of sweatpants, one pair of shorts, one t-shirt, and one sweatshirt at the beginning of each year, but students were notorious for losing their assigned uniform and thus required to buy a new one. Luckily, the storage closet was dry, at least for the time being. Tj grabbed one of each piece of the standard Serenity High School PE uniform and headed for the main office and the teachers' lounge.

She felt somewhat better after changing into dry clothing, but her shoes were soaking wet and her hair was beyond saving. Tj pulled her hair into a sloppy knot, slipped on her wet tennis shoes, and the sloshed to the cafeteria.

"What happened to you?" one of her male students said as she passed.

"Don't ask." Tj looked around the room. Because the locker rooms were closed, the students had been unable to change, which didn't really matter because there was no room to move around anyway. "As you all know," Tj began, "there are broken pipes in the physical education building, so we'll be holding class in here for the time being. Anyone have any suggestions?"

"I have a French test to study for," one of the girls said.

"And I have a math test," another student added.

"Okay, study hall it is," Tj decided.

At least Tj only had three PE classes to teach during the

winter months. As the coach of the downhill team, she spent her afternoons with the team, preparing for the regional competitions. Only three more hours and she'd be on the ski hill and this truly horrible morning would be nothing more than a vague memory.

Or so she hoped.

"What do you mean, the resort is closed?" Tj asked the manager at Angel Mountain, where she and the downhill team practiced.

"Power's out and we can't run the lifts. I spoke to the electric company and they don't think they'll be able to get things up and running until later this afternoon, maybe even this evening. I figured I should call you before you came all the way out here with the kids."

"I appreciate that. I'll have the office make an announcement over the loudspeaker. Please keep me updated; I hope you'll be up and running by tomorrow."

"You and me both. It's going to cost us a pretty penny to be closed for the day. Talk about bad luck. Two weeks ago the conditions were lousy and it wouldn't have been that big of a deal to be closed for a day. Today we have the best conditions we've ever had and we can't get the skiers up the hill."

"The best ever?" Tj groaned.

"The slopes are perfect. Lots of fresh snow, perfectly groomed, plenty of sunshine, and unseasonably warm temperatures. I can't remember the last time it was this perfect."

Tj signed. "Okay, thanks for calling. Let me know about tomorrow."

"Will do."

Tj hung up and headed toward the office. While she had resented being confined to the cafeteria all morning, she found herself hoping it was available for the afternoon. If it wasn't, she wasn't sure what she was going to do with her downhill team. The library was packed with students from the other physical education classes, and as far as she knew, there weren't any open classrooms. Maybe the janitor's closet?

"Thought you'd be headed to the mountain by now," the school secretary commented when Tj walked into the office.

"The resort is closed due to a power outage. Can you make an announcement before anyone leaves?"

"Sure thing. Where should I tell them to meet?" the perky blonde asked.

"Will the cafeteria be available this afternoon?" Tj asked hopefully.

"Sorry, the afternoon PE classes are in there."

"I figured. How about the choir room?" Tj asked.

"Drama club."

"Okay, what do you suggest?" Tj asked.

"They're showing a movie to all the health classes today. Why don't you join them? That will give you a place to meet and something to do."

"Sounds perfect."

"And then," Tj complained to Jake as she drove him to physical therapy later that afternoon, "after I'd already broken the news to my kids that not only were they going to miss the best day of skiing the area has seen in a decade and we were going to have to join the health classes for a movie, I find out that the movie was about the journey your food takes from fork to toilet bowl. It was boring *and* disgusting."

Jake chuckled. "Something on your mind? Something more than flooded offices and boring movies? You aren't usually this prickly."

Tj turned into the parking lot at the hospital, where the therapy sessions were held. "I'm sorry. All I've done is complain from the moment I picked you up. It's just been a really frustrating day, and I didn't sleep all that well last night, so I guess I didn't have the energy I needed to deal with it."

"You don't have to attend the session with me. Once I get inside I can handle it on my own."

"No, I want to come," Tj insisted. "I'll stop whining. We're here to focus on you, and that's what we're going to do. Just let me get the chair."

Tj parked her 4Runner and then jogged around to the back to get the portable wheelchair. She helped Jake into it and then wheeled it inside.

As they were heading toward the bank of elevators that would take them to the second floor, Kyle came walking down the hall with Andrea beside him.

"What happened?" Tj asked the actress, who looked to be sporting a brand-new cast on her arm.

"I slipped on the ice while walking to the limo that arrived earlier to take me to the airport."

"Ouch." Tj grimaced. "I'm so sorry."

Andrea shrugged. "It was my own fault. I should never have been wearing heels. I guess my Paris trip is off for the time being."

"Andi is going to stay with me for a few days while she figures out what she wants to do," Kyle explained.

It sounded like Kyle and Andrea had become more than just a little chummy while she'd been in town.

"Kyle is so sweet." Andrea looked at him adoringly. "He even offered to let me sleep in the master bedroom because it has the best view of the lake."

Yeah, I'll bet he did, Tj thought.

The elevator opened and Tj pushed Jake inside. "I hope your arm doesn't lay you up for too long," Tj offered.

"This may be the painkillers talking, but I'm beginning to think that slipping on the ice was the best thing that's ever happened to me." Andrea grinned.

Tj glanced at Kyle as the elevator doors slid shut. Yup, he had it bad. Tj just hoped that Andrea wouldn't break his heart.

Jake was sent for an X-ray after his session, so Tj decided to visit Stella. Hunter had mentioned the previous evening that she was doing really well and could be released as early as Tuesday. Tj figured she'd offer to pick her up, considering Stella's car was a mangled mess of metal. Stella might need help for the first few days, so she planned to invite her to stay at the resort until she was 100 percent.

"Tj, I'm so glad you're here," Stella said the moment she walked through the door. "Now that I'm awake I'm bored, bored, bored. Do you think you can convince your cute boyfriend to let me out of here before I go insane?"

"I heard you might get out tomorrow. Has anyone talked to you about a release date?" Tj asked.

"The nurses won't say, and Dr. Hanson is being annoyingly vague. I'm going to chuck the doctor's orders and check myself out if they don't let me out of here soon."

"I'll talk to Hunter to see what I can find out. So you're still feeling pretty good?"

"A little sore and I don't have a lot of energy, but I don't need to be in a hospital. I miss Kai, and I bet she's missing me too. I want to go home and finish recovering in my own bed."

Tj pulled out her phone and texted Hunter. If he was in the hospital he'd most likely come by to see how her session with Jake had gone.

"Okay, I texted Hunter. If he shows up before I have to leave to get his grandfather, we can talk to him about getting you out of here. But you need to promise to come out to the resort, where we can help you for a few days."

Stella frowned. "Oh, I don't know. I'd really like to go home."

"I'm not sure you really comprehend how active the puppies are now. There's no way you can take care of them on your own until you get your strength back, and I know you won't want to go home and leave Kai and the puppies with us."

"No," Stella agreed. "I wouldn't want to be home without Kai. Do you have an extra room?"

"Gracie can bunk in with Ashley and you can have her bed. Kai can sleep with you and it will almost be like being at home, only it will be louder and a lot more hectic, but there will be people to help you with the furry little monsters, who have doubled in size while you've been here," Tj teased.

"I guess they would be at that into-everything phase."

"Oh, yeah."

"Okay, but only for a day or two. Just until I feel up to tackling the puppy crew on my own."

Tj turned as Hunter walked through the door with a clipboard in his hand. Hunter glanced at her with a question in his eyes causing Tj to divert her eyes and focus on Stella. "Stella is feeling better, and she's bored staying here, so I'm going to take her home with me."

Tj glanced at Hunter as he frowned but didn't say anything.

"Please, Dr. Hanson," Stella added.

"Yeah, please, Dr. Hanson." Tj tried for her best puppy-dog face. She hated feeling awkward with Hunter so decided to pretend that their disaster of a date never happened.

"And she'll be staying with you?" Hunter clarified.

"She will," Tj promised. "As long as she needs to."

"And you'll follow my instructions and come back on Thursday for a checkup?" he asked Stella.

"I will."

Hunter shrugged. "Okay, let's see about getting you out of here."

Stella clapped her hands and screeched with delight. "You've got yourself a good guy there," she said to Tj.

Tj looked at Hunter with an expression of apology on her face. "Yeah, I do at that."

CHAPTER 11

Later that evening, after Tj had tucked the puppies as well as her sisters into bed and settled Stella in Gracie's room with Kai and a television remote, she headed downstairs to enjoy a few quiet moments and a glass of wine before turning in for the evening. Her father and grandfather were watching a movie on TV, so she settled into the corner of the sofa nearest the warm wood fire and tried to follow along. It seemed like today had been the day that would never end. She was exhausted and really should go to bed, but her mind was trying to process a million different things and refused to give her the calm she needed.

"Stella all tucked in?" her dad asked.

"Yeah. She's watching a sitcom with Kai. She's had a busy evening, so I'd be willing to bet she'll be sound asleep in no time. The girls are tucked into bed and the puppies are in the spare room we set up. I left the door between Gracie's room and the spare room open so Kai can go in and out as needed. How was your date with Rosalie?" Tj knew her dad had taken Rosalie out to a movie and dinner.

"It was nice. Seems like we've both been so busy that it's been a while since we've had time to relax together."

"Yeah, it has been a crazy couple of weeks," Tj agreed as her furry orange cat Cuervo climbed into her lap, turned around in a circle to find the comfiest spot, and then lay down and started to purr. Echo, who was lying at Tj's feet, looked up and glared at the cat before going back to sleep.

"We talked about maybe getting away together when things slow down a bit. Maybe in the spring, before the summer crowds arrive," Mike informed her.

"That sounds nice. Where are you thinking of going?"

"Somewhere warm. Maybe Hawaii. Rosalie is going to see if she can get a friend of hers to come up and cover her practice while she's gone. Being the only veterinarian in town, she hates to close the clinic."

"Let me know what you work out and I'll be happy to do what I can to help out around here," Tj offered.

"Thanks. I appreciate that."

"Speaking of Hawaii, Jenna told me that she and Dennis are trying to plan a trip as well. I told her the girls could stay here with us. I hope that's okay."

"It's absolutely okay. It's good for young couples to take some time for themselves. When are they planning to go?"

"I'm not sure, but I think fairly soon. Dennis worked a ton of overtime during the storm, so Jenna thinks they can swing it financially. Hopefully they can find a window of time that works for both of them with their busy schedules."

"Speaking of busy schedules," Mike said, "I was in town today picking up the mail and some supplies and decided to stop off to order feed for the stables as long as I was there. I got to chatting with Dover Wood, and he mentioned that you'd been nosing around, asking folks about their whereabouts at the time Nolan was murdered."

"I was digging around a bit, but it got me nowhere, and then school started back up today, so I guess I've sort of dropped the ball the past few days. Dover told me he was totally drunk on the day of the murder and didn't remember much of anything."

"Yeah, he told me that too," Mike confirmed, "but he also said something I found interesting."

"What's that?" Tj asked.

Ben turned from the television, which was showing a commercial for denture cream. "Did Dover have a useful clue?"

"I'm not certain how useful this piece of information is," Mike qualified, "but Dover mentioned that he was glad he quit his job with the sheriff's office and opened the feed store. I asked him why he quit in the first place, and he replied that after he became a deputy he'd quickly discovered that the line separating the good guys from the bad guys was often a lot more blurred than he was comfortable with."

"I don't suppose he offered an example of what he meant by that?" Tj asked.

"No. In fact, I could tell by the look on his face that he wished he hadn't said what he had. The thing that struck me as interesting is that just before he made that comment we'd been chatting about Nolan's death and the arson case he'd been looking into. I got the distinct impression he knew something about that case."

"I'm pretty much convinced that the second fire, which was used as an excuse for setting Clay Warner free, was actually set by the deputy who messed up the arrest in the first place," Tj said. "Dennis looked at the fire reports and said that the two fires were similar but far from exactly the same, as Warner's lawyer claimed. It seems like whoever decided that the two fires *were* the same either didn't know what they were talking about or was lying."

"So you think that someone killed Nolan because he'd figured out the truth?" Ben asked.

"I don't know. I kind of doubt it. The four deputies on record as having responded to the fire and subsequently arresting Clay Warner were Dover Wood, Max Stevens, Jerry Johnson, and Jim Boggs. While I think Dover might know something, I really don't think he would kill Nolan over something like that, and Max and Nolan were friends. It seems that if one of these men had set the second fire and Nolan figured it out, Nolan probably wouldn't have acted on the information at this point anyway. What good would it do? Warner is long gone and neither Max nor Dover are still active in law enforcement. Besides, Nolan used to be a cop. I'm sure there's a certain loyalty there, and probably even a certain level of understanding about mistakes being made and covered up."

"So if Nolan wasn't threatening to expose these men, why kill him?" Ben asked.

"Exactly. Now Jerry Johnson and Sheriff Boggs, on the other hand, have a lot more to lose if they're the guilty party and the truth came out. Both are still active in law enforcement, although I hear Jerry is close to retirement. I suppose that a felony conviction could mess up his pension, so he would have a reason to want the truth suppressed, and it would ruin the still-active career of Sheriff Boggs if it were proven that he was guilty of setting the second fire. The thing is, Tim checked with dispatch and neither man left the south shore the entire week of Nolan's murder. At least not during the hours they were on the clock, and both men were on the clock during that time."

"Sounds like you're back to square one," Mike sympathized.

"Basically. I hate to let the only lead we have go, but I'm starting to think the fire and Nolan's murder aren't as closely connected as I first thought. I honestly think I've been busy chasing windmills this past week. First the phone call from Nolan's phone to Murphy's Bar, which may have been nothing more than an intentional distraction, and then the arson cover-up, which I feel certain one or more of the four deputies were involved with. Did Nolan mention anything that was going on that he was worried about or overly focused on during the weeks prior to his death?" Tj asked Ben.

Ben thought about it. "He did seem to have something on his mind, but he never did say exactly what that was. I got the feeling that he was trying to make up his mind about something. He didn't seem worried exactly, but he did seem distracted. And then there was that incident with Kyle, which seemed odd."

"Incident with Kyle?" Tj asked.

"I thought I'd mentioned it. Nolan, Doc, and I were in Murphy's shooting the breeze the day before the storm hit and Kyle walked in with that ad crew that's been in town. He introduced them to everyone, and Nolan got this odd look on his face and insisted on speaking to Kyle privately. I could tell Kyle was uncomfortable about deserting his guests, so he asked Nolan if he could call him later. He even offered to stop by Nolan's house when he was finished with his tour, but Nolan was insistent that Kyle accompany him outside. Kyle agreed to do so after ordering drinks for his guests, but just as Nolan reached the door to leave the bar he stopped and looked at his phone. He turned to Kyle, told him that he'd changed his mind and really needed to go, and left. He didn't even come back over to our table to cover his part of the check."

"Did you ever find out what that was all about?" Tj asked.

"Not really. I didn't hear from Nolan the rest of that day and then the storm hit that night. The first time I talked to him again was the day he was murdered. I asked him about his odd behavior in the bar and he apologized. He said he got a text about a cold case he was working on. He said he still needed to fit together a couple more pieces and needed to talk to someone before he was ready to go public with what he'd found out. After that he started chatting about cold cases in general, which led to our discussion of the fire. I have to admit I was pretty focused on that particular cold case because Nolan seemed pretty excited about something he'd learned. He was about to tell me what that was when whoever killed him showed up at the door. I guess I figured that because that was the one he was talking about when he died, the fire was the case that got him killed, but I suppose the killer might be linked with one of the others."

"Or something else entirely," Mike pointed out.

"Maybe," Tj acknowledged. "But Nolan was well liked in the community. Other than his delving into cold cases, I don't know what else he might have been into that could have got him killed. Besides, unless someone knows something I don't, the cold cases are the only leads we have."

"So other than the fire that killed that young couple and

the subsequent fire that allowed the killer to go free, what was he working on?" Mike asked.

"Kyle and Roy both mentioned that Nolan was dealing with files regarding the fires, the second body in the old lady's grave, and an old discharge of firearms conviction that concerned a minor and a gun stolen from the armory at the shooting range."

Tj went over what she could remember from each of the cases with the men who were present.

"Too bad the file on the minor is sealed," Ben commented. "Still, I don't see how something like that could get Nolan killed. I'm sure those guns walk away more often than anyone would like to admit."

"Yeah, that's what Tim said. It seems unlikely that a stolen gun fifteen years ago would lead to Nolan's death," Tj agreed. "As for the second body in the coffin, I suppose if Nolan figured out who the body belonged to and who put it there, that might be a reason for someone to want him dead."

"You think he could have figured that out after all this time?" Ben asked.

"Maybe," Tj answered. "Nolan was a smart guy, and he knew what to look for. If anyone could figure it out it would be him."

"Maybe we should ask Doc to take a look at the remains," Ben suggested. "As a former Orange County coroner, Doc has a lot more experience than our local coroners and the technology used to identify remains has improved significantly since the body was initially found.

Tj realized Ben had a good idea. It seemed like a long shot, but he was a very accomplished coroner. Maybe he could figure out a way to identify the body even though there were no dental records or fingerprints to refer to. If they could identify the victim maybe they could identify the killer.

"I'll talk to Roy about getting him access to the remains if you think he'd be willing to take a look at them."

"I'll call him in the morning," Ben promised.

"I'm sure Roy and Tim will appreciate the help," Tj said. "I got the feeling when I spoke to both men that they are in over their heads with this one. They both seemed really stressed."

"And what about you?" Ben asked.

Tj shrugged. "I don't know. I'm out of ideas and I do have classes to teach, a regional snowboard competition to win, sisters to raise, and a really important decision to make. Yeah, I guess you could say that I'm stressed."

CHAPTER 12

Friday, March 20

The second body in the coffin was Clay Warner. Tj would never have guessed that in a million years. For one thing, almost everyone had been operating under the assumption that the body had been placed in the coffin long after Warner had fled the area. For another, whoever had killed him knew how to make a body disappear. The question remained, who would want the man gone badly enough to go through all that trouble? If the person who set the second fire, which resulted in Warner's release, turned around and killed him, that might give Nolan a much stronger reason to see him brought to justice.

"Coach Jensen?" Tj realized Stephanie was standing in front of her, as if waiting for an answer to a question she hadn't heard. "Do you want us to head up the mountain again?"

Tj looked around. The downhill team had completed their drills and were waiting for further instructions. "No, I think we're done for today. We should be able to resume our regular training schedule next week. The weather forecast is calling for sunny days, and Mr. Remington told me we should be able to reopen the physical education building. I appreciate everyone's patience with all the changes this week. Have a good weekend and I'll see you on Monday."

"Do you know if Ms. Blake will be back soon?" Stephanie asked about Stella. "The sub is really bad and I'm afraid we're going to fall behind."

"I'm not sure," Tj told her. "She's doing better and plans to return to her own home in a few days, but my guess is that she'll be away from work for another few weeks at least. I'll see what I can find out and update everyone on Monday. I know she appreciates the supportive emails many of you have sent, and I'm sure she's as anxious to get back to teaching as you are to have her back."

"It's been really hard for some of us with Ms. Weston quitting right in the middle of the year and now this happening to Ms. Blake. You aren't planning on going anywhere, are you?"

Tj smiled. "No, I'm afraid you're stuck with me."

Math teacher Nikki Weston had gone home for Christmas, rekindled an old love affair, and decided to stay. The whole thing had been as much of a shock to Tj as it had been to her students and the high school administration. The last Tj'd heard, she was somewhere in Europe with her new fiancé.

"We're happy to be stuck with you." Stephanie hugged Tj. "I wanted to thank you again for working it out for Oliver and me to help with the commercial. It was *so* fun and Andrea was so nice."

"You guys did a great job." Tj began gathering her things. Most of the team had wandered away, but Stephanie seemed to want to chat. "I can't wait to see how it turns out. Everyone I've talked to thinks it's going to be really awesome."

"My counselor thinks it will look good on my college applications," Stephanie said. "Apparently taking AP classes and maintaining a 4.0 GPA isn't enough to get into the really good colleges anymore. She said you need to have a well-rounded portfolio with a variety of activities. I've been losing sleep going over everything in my head. I really need a scholarship."

"You're only a sophomore," Tj pointed out. "It seems like you're way ahead of most students at this point. You're a good student, you participate in two sports, and you're on the student council. Any college would be lucky to have you."

"Maybe. But I've been thinking about joining the choir. Do you know if Kyle is going to help out again next year?"

Technically, Tj was the staff member assigned to the school's newly developed show choir, but Kyle had volunteered to help her out and she had given him the horse along with the reins. While Tj couldn't carry a tune in a bucket, Kyle had a long background in music, and the kids loved him.

"As far as I know," Tj answered, "although I haven't specifically asked him about it."

Tj knew Kyle loved being the choir director, but she couldn't help but wonder how his new relationship with Andrea Washburn was going to affect *everything*. Tj and Kyle were normally inseparable, but other than a brief conversation on the phone on Wednesday, she hadn't talked to him all week. She had heard, however, that Andrea was still staying at his place and was going to remain in town at least through the weekend.

"I hope he does," Stephanie said as Tj began her trek toward the parking lot. "The choir did really well this year, and everyone is saying that next year should be even better. I wouldn't want to waste my time participating in a group that never wins anything."

"I promise I'll talk to Kyle about it when I get the chance, and I'll let you know what he's thinking before you join."

"Thanks. I appreciate that."

Tj opened the back door of her SUV and placed her snowboard inside. Then she slipped off her jacket and tossed it onto the backseat. "Do you need a ride?" Tj asked.

"No, my mom is coming to get me." The teenager looked around. "In fact, she's over there by the entrance. I'll see you Monday."

With that, Stephanie trotted off and Tj started her car. She turned on the heater and defroster, then stopped to check her messages while the car thawed out. The parking lot of the ski resort was beginning to empty out as the sun dipped behind the distant mountain peak, dropping the temperature a good ten degrees. Given the fact that it was Friday, Tj knew that a lot of the vehicles still in the icy parking lot belonged to weekend visitors who had moved to the bar.

There were two messages from her grandpa, asking her if she would be able to take him into town that evening to attend the Friday night poker game at the senior center. She texted back that she would be happy to take him as soon as she got home. There was a text from Ashley, asking if she and Gracie could spend the night at Jenna's. Tj texted Jenna to make sure she knew about the plans the girls had made and then let Ashley know that they'd talk about it when she got home. And there was a text from Hunter, asking if she wanted to go out that evening, and one from Roy, saying they needed to talk.

Tj texted Hunter to tell him she'd call him after she got home and then dialed Roy's cell.

"What's up?" she asked.

"I was going through the files Kyle managed to retrieve from Nolan's place for the hundredth time, trying to see if there was any small piece of information that might help us with our current investigation, and I found something interesting."

"Interesting how?" Tj asked as she nibbled on the end of a protein bar.

"Nolan had a file regarding the original fire in which the couple was killed. He'd somehow managed to find out there was a third resident of the house who wasn't home at the time of the fire."

"Oh, and who was that?" Tj asked as she picked a piece of nut out of her teeth.

"I had to do some digging since the name was not immediately available. I went back through some handwritten notes stuffed into a file Nolan had and learned that the female victim's sister was living with them at the time. You'll never guess what her name is."

Tj sat forward. "Andrea Washburn."

"How did you know?" Roy sounded disappointed that Tj already knew his big news.

"I didn't until right now. I could tell by the build-up you gave your news that it was important, and then I remembered that Andrea had told me she only lived in Serenity for a couple of years. She'd said she moved in with her sister after her mother died, and then she went to live with an aunt when her sister passed as well a couple of years later. Somehow everything just clicked. What do you think this means?"

"I'm not sure," Roy admitted.

Tj sat back in her car seat and chewed on the tip of her nail. "Grandpa said Nolan told him he had news about the fire but that he needed to talk to someone first. Do you think that someone was Andrea?"

"Your guess is as good as mine, although according to Nolan's notes, Andrea was on a date when the fire occurred, so I'm not sure how she'd have any information we don't already have."

Tj bit her lip. "Yeah, it does seem pretty cut and dried, despite the fact that we don't really *know* any more than we did when we started this investigation."

"So Andrea was out on a date," Roy reviewed. "Clay Warner comes to the house to talk to the new owners about returning the cabin he believes is rightfully his. They refuse. He goes ballistic, ties them up, and then burns down the house with materials he finds on the property. At some point after that, Warner is arrested by deputies Boggs, Johnson, Wood, and Stevens. A mistake of some sort is made during the arrest that causes the district attorney to question his ability to prosecute the case. Emotions are high, it's a very high-profile case, so one or more of the four men who participated in the arrest set a copycat fire at an abandoned building. Warner's defense attorney uses the second fire as a defense for his client and Warner is set free. Then someone, probably whoever was responsible for the copycat fire, kills Warner, mutilates and dismembers the body so as to leave it unrecognizable, and then places it in the coffin of Estella Goodwin, whose burial was delayed due to flooding."

"Sounds like a theory," Tj agreed.

"So what piece of information do you think Nolan suspected Andrea might have if he did indeed want to speak to her?" Roy asked.

Tj paused to think about it. She couldn't imagine how horrible it must have been for a teenage Andrea Washburn to learn that the only living member of her immediate family had been brutally murdered while she was on a date. Tj had to wonder why Andrea had even come back to Serenity. She remembered that Andrea had specifically requested to be part of the commercial, so she must have considered the commercial an opportunity to return to the area. But why would she want to come back to a place where such a horrible thing had happened? Unless...

"What if the cop or cops who set the fire didn't kill Clay Warner?" Tj asked.

"Then who did it?"

"Think about it. Who would Warner's release affect the most?"

"I guess the family of the victims. You're saying Andrea Washburn killed Clay Warner," Roy stated. "Maybe Nolan figured it out, so he contacted Andrea to talk to her about it, she realized he was on to her, and she came to Serenity to clean up loose ends."

"It makes sense," Tj said.

"It seems like a long shot. How would a kid like Andrea Washburn know how to do to Warner's body what was done to it? And how did she gain access to Estella Goodwin's coffin?"

"Maybe she had help," Tj insisted.

"Okay, then, who helped her?"

"I don't know."

"Maybe I should bring her in and talk to her," Roy suggested.

"And if she denies everything? We don't have any proof *at all*. In fact, all we do have is an admittedly wild theory. If we spook Andrea, what's to keep her from just taking off? She has access to a private plane," Tj told Roy. "Besides, Kyle will be furious if we accuse her of this horrible crime with absolutely no proof."

"Why will Kyle be furious?" Roy asked. "He's helped us build theories before. He knows how it's done."

"I think he's in love with her." Tj sighed. "She's been staying at his house all week. Oh, God, she's at his house!" Tj realized. "Kyle is sleeping with a killer. We need to do something!"

"Hold on," Roy cautioned. "We don't *know* that she's guilty of the gruesome act we just assigned to her. You were right in the first place; we need more. If she's guilty we don't want to tip her off. And if Kyle does have a thing for her, you need to be careful about what you tell him. Guys in lust usually demonstrate no discernable common sense."

"Yeah." Tj took a deep breath. "You're right. We need to find some sort of proof that Andrea killed Clay Warner—if she did indeed kill him. Question is, where do we start?"

Tj could hear Roy rustling the papers on his desk. She figured he was taking another look at everything. They had managed to gather together all the files and paperwork available through the county records, but the truth of what had happened would most likely be found in Nolan's notes, not the official paperwork. Unfortunately, Kyle had Nolan's computer, as well as his notes. As far as Tj knew, Andrea might have used the access to his home to destroy any proof that might have existed if she really did kill Clay Warner and hide his body in Estella Goodwin's coffin.

As odd as it might sound, Tj wouldn't really blame Andrea for doing what she did, if she'd actually done it. Tj couldn't imagine how furious she would be if someone she loved was brutally murdered and the man who'd killed her loved one was set free. Still, it looked like they were back to square one. Again.

"If you aren't busy tonight, why don't you come over to Hunter's? He doesn't know it yet, but I'm going to suggest we meet at his house while our grandpas are playing poker. My sisters are staying overnight at Jenna's, so I should be free the entire evening."

"I'm not busy. What time do you want me to come over?" Roy asked.

"Let me call you back after I talk to Jenna and Hunter. I'm going to head home now to change and pick up Grandpa, so give me twenty minutes or so to get back to you. Gather together all the files and paperwork you have and bring it with you. We can pick up pizza to nibble on while we work."

"Sounds good. I'll be waiting for your call."

"Oh and bring Tim along if he is available."

"He has his big date tonight."

"Oh yeah. Okay then you can just fill him in later. I'll talk to you soon."

Luckily, Hunter was fine with spending the evening

theorizing and Jenna confirmed that she'd invited the girls to spend the night. A couple of Stella's friends had come by to visit her, so Tj didn't need to feel guilty about leaving her alone while Ben was playing poker and her dad was out with Rosalie.

CHAPTER 13

It seemed so odd to dig into a theory-building and fact-finding session without Kyle. In every investigation Tj had undertaken, with the exception of the first one, Kyle had been right there beside her, making sense of facts that hadn't always been easy to figure out. If Kyle knew she was intentionally leaving him out, he'd be hurt. On the other hand, if he discovered that his new girlfriend was their prime suspect, he'd be more than hurt.

"I don't see how we're going to figure this out without the rest of the files that are still on Nolan's computer," Hunter commented, then turned to Roy. "Maybe you can ask Kyle to turn the computer over to you?"

"I can, but he's going to wonder why I'm asking for it. He knows I don't have the technical skill to find whatever it is Nolan may have hidden on that hard drive. Besides, I know Kyle has been looking into Nolan's death. If he'd found anything relevant, he would have told me."

"So we're assuming Kyle didn't read Nolan's handwritten notes?" Hunter asked.

"No, I don't think he did," Roy answered. "He gave me

the files he found but didn't indicate he'd read them. He planned to concentrate on the hard drive."

"Then maybe there isn't anything about Andrea on the hard drive," Hunter said. "If Kyle came across a reference to Andrea in Nolan's computer files, I would think he'd have said something to us about it."

"Unless he's protecting her," Roy commented.

"He wouldn't do that," Tj insisted. "At least not if he had reason to believe she was really guilty. Maybe I'm not giving him enough credit. Maybe if we called him right now and told him what we suspected, he'd look at our theory objectively and realize that maybe we're on to something."

"Or maybe he wouldn't," Roy said. "I think telling him at this point might be an unnecessary risk. If nothing else, he might start acting differently around Andrea, and that could tip her off. We don't want her to run before we figure this out."

Tj knew Roy was right, but she still didn't like it. Eventually, Kyle was going to find out that they'd excluded him from the investigation, and the last thing she wanted to do was hurt the man who had become like a brother to her.

"Maybe we can find out who Andrea's boyfriend was," Tj suggested. "If she did kill Warner she must have had help, and maybe it was the boyfriend who helped her."

"You did say she was on a date the night of the murder," Hunter said to Roy. "Does the report mention who she was with?"

Roy looked through the paperwork once again. "No. It just says she was on a date."

"Rob said Andrea was part of a clique in high school," Tj commented. "A Goth group. Maybe if we can figure out who she hung out with we can find someone who might be able to answer the question."

"The murder happened fifteen years ago. How are we going to figure out who Andrea hung out with unless we ask her?" Roy asked.

"Wait," Tj said at the same moment. "Brandon Halliwell. Rob said Brandon Halliwell used to have a thing for Andrea. I can't believe I didn't remember that. We need to talk to Brandon."

"The store is already closed for the day," Roy pointed out. "I could track him down, but it's Friday night and I'd be willing to bet he's out with the guys. I suppose this can wait until tomorrow."

"Yeah, it can wait," Tj agreed. "If it wasn't Brandon, and he doesn't know who it was she was dating at the time of the murder, Rob has a yearbook that shows who attended Serenity High School at the same time Andrea did. I'm sure we can borrow it and then talk to those students who still live in the area."

"I'll drop by to talk to Rob either way," Roy said. "If there's one thing I've learned by doing this my entire working life, it's that the more people you talk to the more perspectives you're likely to pick up."

"Call me after you talk to Brandon," Tj requested.

Roy nodded. "Thanks for the pizza, but I'm beat. I think I'm going to head home. I have a feeling it's going to be a busy weekend."

After Roy left, Hunter opened a bottle of wine and the couple settled in to spend a few quiet moments together before Tj had to go pick up Ben from the poker game. Hunter's home was much larger than the house she lived in with her family, but it was equally warm and cozy.

When he decided to buy the lakefront home he'd looked for something that could comfortably provide shelter and privacy for both himself and his grandfather, who he didn't want living alone after the heart attack he'd suffered several years earlier. His sister Chelsea had lived with them for a while as well, but she'd moved to the East Coast the previous winter, after her ex had been murdered and she'd been, for a time, the prime suspect.

Tj snuggled into Hunter's side on the overstuffed sofa. He put his arm around her and she leaned her head against his chest. "This is nice."

"Really nice," Hunter agreed. "It's been a while since we've had much alone time. I miss us."

"Speaking of alone time," Tj began, "I've been thinking about a trip."

"A trip?"

"Dennis and Jenna are going to Hawaii and Dad is taking Rosalie somewhere tropical during the off season, and it got me thinking about how nice it would be for you and me to take a trip together. Just the two of us."

"That sounds wonderful, but what about the girls?"

"I'm sure between Dad, Grandpa, and Jenna I can work out childcare. It would have to be after school is out because we're already so short-staffed at the high school. There's no way I could request time off. I'd like to be home to help Dad during the busiest part of the summer, so maybe the second half of June?"

Hunter tucked a stray lock of her hair behind her ear.

"June might work. I'll need to contact the traveling doctors program to see if I can get a sub. I have doctors I can leave in charge, but I'll need the extra hands if we're going to be away during the summer, when things tend to be hectic anyway. I'll call them tomorrow to see what I can work out. How long were you thinking?"

"Two weeks," Tj said hopefully.

"Should be doable. Any thoughts as to where you want to go?"

"Somewhere tropical," Tj asserted. "I'm thinking hiking and surfing during the day and long walks on a warm moonlight beach at night."

"Sounds wonderful." Hunter kissed her neck.

"Remember when we were in high school and we used to talk about taking a year off before college to sail around the world?" Tj asked.

Hunter laughed. "Yeah. I guess that was a little impractical."

"Maybe, and to be honest, I wouldn't want to spend that much time on the water anyway, but besides being impractical it was romantic and adventurous. Sometimes I feel like I slipped into middle age and never even knew it was happening. It'd be fun to do something fun and romantic, with just a hint of danger. No actual danger, mind you—I do have the girls to consider—but maybe something with just a whisper of the unknown."

Hunter traced his finger over her shoulder and down her arm. "I guess we could do something like white-water rafting or scuba diving. I had a friend who went on a treasure hunt."

"A treasure hunt?" Tj asked.

"It was a fake treasure hunt, with real clues but a fake

map and a fake treasure. He spent four days camping in the desert, but he said it was fun."

"Yeah, but maybe not camping, and definitely not the desert. I like the idea of scuba diving though, and I love to hike as long as I have a nice soft bed to hike back to at the end of the day."

"Tj Jensen, I do believe you've gone and turned into a girl," Hunter teased.

"Yeah, I guess I have." Tj laughed. Teenage Tj would have been all over the camping.

"Let me check the vacation schedule at the hospital and see about getting a sub and then we can talk dates. I guess I should consider what to do about Grandpa as well. As little as a week ago, I would have worried that he wouldn't be able to get around on his own, but it seems you're some sort of miracle worker. He's sticking to his diet and doing every single one of the exercises the physical therapist recommended without even the slightest complaint. I have a feeling he'll be walking on his own in no time."

"We had a heart-to-heart and he agreed to try his best," Tj informed Hunter.

"Well, whatever you said was inspired. He's like a different person." Hunter kissed her on the lips. "You, my dear, are a genius. It's like he has a new lease on life."

CHAPTER 14

Saturday, March 21

"I have to say I'm more than just a little frustrated," Tj complained as she sat at the counter in the kitchen of the Antiquery and whined to Jenna while she made breakfast for her customers.

Dennis had taken all four girls sledding, so Tj ended up having a free day, and evidently complaining to Jenna was the most important thing she could think of to do with her newly found free time.

"I'm sure Hunter will work things out. Just give him some time. He has a hard job to find coverage for."

"I know, but after we talked last night I was really excited for us to get away together, and then he calls me this morning and tells me that the traveling doctors group doesn't have any subs for the end of June. I can't go away until school is out, and it's so busy at the resort during July and August that I hate to leave Dad without enough help."

Jenna poured perfectly round pancakes on the grill. Tj

had been eyeing the warm berry compote her friend had been using to top the pancakes. If things slowed down a bit, she might have Jenna make her a couple of the golden cakes.

"Maybe if Hunter can't find anyone to cover in late June you can find someone to help your dad in July or August. I know the resort is busy and you'd feel guilty, but I'm sure he wants you and Hunter to have the time you need."

"Time we need for what?" Tj asked.

Jenna didn't say anything.

"You think my dad wants Hunter and me to move things along in the relationship department?"

"Honey, I think your dad wants you to be happy, and yeah, I think he thinks that in the long run Hunter will make you happy."

"You told me to be sure I was ready to accept the whole package before moving the relationship forward," Tj reminded her.

"I did."

"I've thought about that. A lot. I'm not saying I'm ready to walk down the aisle, but I do think I'm ready to make a commitment of sorts."

Jenna smiled. "I'm glad. I've always thought you and Hunter belonged together."

"And yet you were one of the few people who's been warning me to take it slow and be sure about how I feel."

Jenna slid the golden cakes onto a plate and covered them with the berries and a shake of powdered sugar. "Relationships are complicated. Even when you love the person you're in the relationship with more than life itself. Even in the best of circumstances, marriage can test your commitment to each other. I can't imagine surviving the difficult times if your commitment to the relationship wasn't solid to begin with."

"You are a wise woman, Jenna Elston."

Jenna slid the plate of hot cakes in front of her. "You want me to deliver these?" Tj asked.

"They're for you. I noticed the little hint of drool in the corner of your mouth."

"I don't drool," Tj countered. "But thank you. I was coveting them and I *am* hungry."

Tj sliced off a large bite and chewed slowly, enjoying the combination of sweet and tart. Jenna pulled the next order off the wire and began preparing the eggs that were the center of the omelet-based entrée.

"So how are things going in your investigation into Nolan's murder?" Jenna asked as she added diced meat and veggies to the eggs.

"Honestly? I'm not getting anywhere. I keep thinking we're moving forward, but then things loop back around to the exact spot where we started and we're no further along than we were the day Nolan was killed."

"It's a complicated case involving another complicated case that was never solved," Jenna pointed out. "Sometimes these things take time."

"Yeah, and sometimes they never wind up being solved." Tj groaned. "The thing is, last night everything seemed to make perfect sense. All we needed was for Brandon to fill in the blanks and give us something to take to the bank, but then he told Roy that he wasn't even in town the night of the fire and had no idea who Andrea was out with. He claims to have been on some sort of backpack trip with his friends."

"And you don't believe him?" Jenna asked.

Tj shrugged. "I don't know. I guess I don't have any reason not to believe him, but there's something that just isn't lining up about this whole thing."

"Maybe Roy should just talk to Andrea. It seems like she may be the only one who knows what really happened."

"Yeah, but if she's guilty she's never going to admit it, and telling her that we suspect her will give her the opportunity to take off before she can be arrested."

"Based on the chatter from the Serenity gossip hotline, Andrea plans to leave the area on Monday anyway. Harriet mentioned that she overheard Clinton the cab guy talking to Andrea about taking her to the airport Monday morning. It seems to me that you have less than forty-eight hours to figure this out."

Tj frowned. "Why wouldn't Andrea just have Kyle take her to the airport?"

"That I do not know."

Tj got up from the stool she was sitting on and refilled her coffee. She needed to make sure that *all* her brain cells were functioning at 100 percent. "When did Harriet overhear the conversation between Clinton and Andrea?"

"I'm not sure. I guess you could call Harriet to ask her."

"I will."

Tj called Harriet, who told her that her car was in the shop so she'd hired Clinton to bring her into town. Although it was Saturday and her day off, she'd wanted to get caught up on her paperwork, and she had an appointment with the hairdresser later in the afternoon. Clinton received the call from Andrea while she was chatting with him just after they'd arrived at the county offices. Harriet reported that Clinton was over-the-moon excited to have the opportunity to drive

Andrea Washburn to the airport, which was a good hour and a half away, and he made sure he told everyone within hearing distance about his upcoming excursion.

"It sounds like Andrea called Clinton about a half hour after Roy talked to Brandon. Do you think Brandon warned her?" Tj asked Jenna when she'd shared what she'd learned from Harriet.

Jenna cracked several eggs into a pan. "I guess he could have. If what Rob said was true, it sounds like Brandon had a thing for Andrea in high school, whether she returned his affection or not. He might feel inclined to warn her if he thought she was in trouble."

"I need to talk to Roy."

"You should talk to Kyle," Jenna counseled.

"You think so? What if he's mad?"

"Then he's mad, but Kyle has the most level head on his shoulders of any person I've ever met. Maybe he's in love with Andrea and maybe he isn't, but either way he's a smart guy, and once you tell him what you figured out he's going to see that Andrea is a viable suspect. Maybe he can help you. Maybe he can talk to her, or maybe he can find the proof you need in Nolan's paperwork. You don't have a lot of time to prove your theory. I think that whether you want to or not you're going to need to trust Kyle to do the right thing."

Tj thought about what Jenna had said. She was right; Kyle was a good guy who wouldn't turn his back on finding out the truth about Nolan's murder no matter how he might feel about the prime murder suspect. Tj called Roy to tell him that Andrea had plans to leave town and then called Kyle to ask if they could meet. Alone. He, of course, had no idea what was going on, so he gladly invited her to stop by.

* * *

When Tj arrived at Kyle's house he showed her into the computer room, which had been built with extra insulation and so was virtually soundproof. He had a table set up with the computer he had taken from Nolan's the day after his murder. He apologized for not having had as much time to work on the murder as he would have liked before offering her a seat at the table.

"So have you found something?" he asked.

"I think we may have a new suspect based on a theory we worked up after receiving some new information," Tj nervously began.

"Okay, shoot. What do you have?"

"It seems there was a third person living in the cabin that burned down in the first fire: the female victim's sister. She was a high school student out on a date that evening."

Kyle sat quietly while he waited for Tj to come to a point.

"The third resident was Andrea Washburn."

Kyle frowned. "Andrea? Are you sure?"

"Yeah, I'm sure."

"I wonder why she hasn't said anything," Kyle said. "That must have been horrible for her."

"I can't even imagine," Tj agreed. "If someone I loved was brutally murdered and then the killer was set free I don't know what I'd do."

Kyle looked Tj in the eye. "What are you getting at?"

"There's more. The second body in Estella Goodwin's coffin belonged to Clay Warner. Doc verified it this week. We believe someone killed Warner after he was set free and then put him in the coffin."

"You think Andrea killed Clay?" Kyle seemed shocked but not angry. Tj supposed being shocked was better than being mad.

"It makes sense. Heck, if it had been me, I might have killed Clay Warner. What he did to her sister was brutal and ugly. If you ask me, he deserved to die," Tj asserted. "Nolan, however, didn't."

Kyle furrowed his brow. "You think Andrea killed Nolan?"

"I hope not, but someone did, and it makes sense that *someone* killed him to keep him from revealing what he'd found out."

"No," Kyle decided. "I can almost buy that Andrea was involved with Clay Warner's death, but there's no way she killed Nolan. I know you haven't had a chance to really get to know her, but she's a good person. She would never kill Nolan for figuring out the truth even if she was guilty of something. We need to ask her what happened with Clay. If she's guilty of avenging her sister's death, I'll get her the best lawyer in the country."

"Are you sure?" Tj asked. "You've only just met her."

"I'm sure," Kyle declared.

Kyle brought Andrea into the room and filled her in on the information they'd found, as well as Tj's suspicions about her involvement in Clay Warner's murder. She began to sob as Kyle gently revealed the theory to her, leading Tj to guess that she was, indeed, guilty.

"It's not what you think," she cried. "Yes, I wanted Clay to pay for what he did to my sister, and yes, I know who killed him, but I didn't actually do it. How could I? I was a kid. A very scared and lost kid who'd just lost the only person in the world who meant anything to her. I could barely function, let alone come up with a plan to kill and dismember the man I hated above all others."

Kyle gave her a tissue and then took her hand. The tenderness with which he was treating her left no doubt in Tj's mind that things had progressed way beyond the acquaintanceship stage between them.

"When I heard Clay was going to be released I went nuts. Who wouldn't? I had spent every moment of my life from the time I learned how my sister died imagining her last moments on this earth. To be tied to the man you loved in the middle of a building you knew was going to burn must have been beyond horrifying. My sister was a good person. She didn't deserve to die that way. No one does."

Andrea took a deep breath.

"I was with some friends when I heard he'd been released, and hard as they tried to comfort me, I was inconsolable. I was crying and screaming about the unfairness of the situation. This man had brutally killed my sister and now he was going to be able to live out his life with no consequences. I was insane with grief and shouted that the man needed to die. I said that if anyone really wanted to do something to help me they would make sure the man did die."

"Someone killed Clay for you?" Tj said.

"Yes, but I didn't know until afterward. One of my friends came to me and told me he had shot Clay and then cut him into small pieces. He told me that he'd put the remains in a dead woman's coffin. I was horrified, but I realized it was my fault. I had asked for someone to kill this man and one dear friend actually had. I knew it was wrong, but how could I tell? I moved away a few days later and went to live with my aunt. I've never told anyone."

"Who was it?" Kyle asked.

Andrea hesitated. "Do you really want to send this man to jail for killing that monster? I happen to know he grew up to be a good man."

"He might have killed Nolan," Tj said.

Andrea frowned as she thought about that. "It's hard to believe he would."

"Someone did," Tj pointed out.

Andrea buried her face in her hands. "I need to think. Once I say something it can't be unsaid. Surely you have other suspects."

Kyle looked at Tj. She shrugged.

"Here's everything we know," Kyle began. He filled Andrea in on the facts concerning all three cases they knew Nolan was working on.

"The killer has to be one of the four deputies," Andrea insisted.

"Maybe," Kyle acknowledged, "but I feel like we've pretty much cleared them all."

"What about the third case—the one with the stolen gun?" Andrea asked.

"We haven't really found out much at all about that one," Tj admitted.

"I'll tell you what: let's keep looking. Let's make sure that every option has been explored and eliminated. In the end, if it comes back to Clay Warner's murder, I'll tell you who did it. But if we find, as I suspect we will, that someone else killed Nolan, I'll take the secret with me."

Kyle looked at Tj. She lifted an eyebrow. She was certain

neither of them really wanted to see Clay Warner's killer imprisoned unless he was the one responsible for Nolan's death.

"Okay," Tj agreed. "For now, we'll continue to look, but I need your word that if the evidence comes back around to the person you're protecting, you'll tell us who it is."

"I promise," Andrea said.

"Okay, let's get to work. We need to figure out why Nolan was investigating the gun theft," Kyle stated.

"I know he was at the shooting range, which is where the armory is located, on the day before the storm," Tj said. "Hazel said he was writing in a small notebook."

"So we need to find that notebook," Kyle stated the obvious.

"I suppose we can go back to his house and look around. I feel like I should bring Roy into our investigation. He's been so great about sharing with me to this point," Tj said.

"We can't tell the cops," Andrea insisted.

"How about if we just tell Roy we're going to dig into the gun theft and the case against the minor for illegally discharging a gun and leave the facts surrounding Clay's murder out of it for now?" Tj suggested.

Both Kyle and Andrea agreed. They decided that Andrea would wait at the house while Kyle and Tj went over to Nolan's.

CHAPTER 15

"I think we both suspect who killed Clay Warner," Tj said to Kyle as they drove toward the shooting range. They'd decided at the last minute to ask the deputy in charge what Nolan had asked him about on the day before the storm.

"Brandon Halliwell."

"The fact that I can't imagine him killing Nolan is the main reason I agreed to this crazy plan," Tj commented. "Still, Brandon knows how to shoot, he's been hunting since he was five and knows how to skin an animal—or a person, in the case of Warner—and he has now and had then the tools to dismember a body, whether animal or human. And he's tall and strong and physically capable of killing both Clay and Nolan. I think we need to keep that in mind."

"I agree." Kyle turned into the parking lot. "You did say that he was at Murphy's at the time of the murder."

"Actually, he said he was in and out and might have come in after the call when I spoke to him."

"You don't think...?"

"God, I hope not." Tj sighed.

They parked and made their way inside the stone building, which not only housed the county armory but provided a row of individual booths that could be used for target practice, as well as a larger structure in the back with rooms that were used for training purposes. The site served the entire county, including the north and south shores of Paradise Lake. Private gun enthusiasts could also pay to use the shooting range when it wasn't in use for official purposes.

"Are you here to shoot?" the guy at the desk asked. He looked like he wasn't much more than a kid, but Tj knew that all new recruits started at the armory while they trained to be deputy sheriffs.

"Actually, we just have a few questions, if you don't mind," Tj began.

The kid looked suspicious but agreed to listen to her request.

"I guess you knew Nolan Rivers?"

"Sure. He was here to shoot every week. He was good too."

"Was he in the day before the big storm hit?" Tj wondered.

"Why are you asking?"

"We're helping Roy and Tim investigate Nolan's death. The two of them have been so busy with everything that's been going on, and being shorthanded and all..."

"I'll need to call to check with them before answering any questions about Nolan," the kid insisted.

Tj shrugged. "Sure. Go ahead. We can wait."

The young recruit called Roy, who told him it was fine to talk to them.

"Okay, yeah, he was here. He didn't come in to shoot that day though. He wanted to ask some questions, and he asked for access to some old files I didn't even know we had."

"Did you let him look at the files?" Tj asked.

"Sure. He used to be a cop. I trusted him."

"So what exactly was he asking about?" Tj wondered.

"He was looking for some information about one of the cold cases he was working on. He liked to poke around in those unsolved crimes. We used to chat about them from time to time. Anyway, it seems there were some guns stolen from the armory long before my time and he was looking into it."

"Did he find what he was looking for?" Tj asked.

The kid shrugged. "I don't know. I let him into the room he wanted access to and then came back to the desk. To be honest, the case seemed sort of boring. Who cares if some guns went missing fifteen years ago? Guns go missing all the time. We don't like to advertise that, but it's a fact and Nolan knew it, so I don't know why he was so interested in those particular guns."

"Do you think you can show us to the files he was looking at?" Kyle asked.

"I don't suppose it would hurt. Don't take nothing though. Just my luck that someone else would come looking for those old files and they'd be gone."

"Did anyone other than Nolan want to see the files?" Tj asked.

"Just Tim Matthews."

Tj realized that Tim must have been investigating along the same lines that she and Kyle had.

"So what are we looking for?" Kyle asked as he opened a box on the top of the pile.

"I wish I knew."

Tj started looking through the boxes of paperwork. Most

of them contained the logs that kept track of who checked out a gun and the times it was checked in and out. Tj realized that the boxes had dates on the outside, so she searched for the appropriate year. She took the box from the stack and opened the lid. It looked as if most of the paperwork was missing. Tj frowned.

"This box is mostly empty," Tj commented.

"What if the guns were stolen by the clerk who worked at the armory at the time?" Kyle hypothesized. "If you look at these logs, they really had a pretty loose system. Everything was logged in and out by hand."

"I guess it would be easy for the clerk to steal the guns," Tj admitted. "So who was the clerk at the time the guns went missing?"

Kyle looked at the few logs that were left in the box. "There are eight months' worth of logs missing. I'm willing to bet whoever the clerk was who worked in the armory during that time is our gun thief. The sign-in logs are missing, but I bet I can find out who we're looking for through the county pay records."

"Back to your house?"

"Let's go ahead and continue on to Nolan's," Kyle said. "Maybe we can find the notebook and his notes will save me the trouble of hacking into the county records."

Kyle and Tj drove to Nolan's in silence. Tj suspected they were both afraid of what they would find. Sometimes solving a crime meant uncovering facts about a friend that you'd just as soon rather not know.

They parked on the street and made their way through the snow to the front door. Kyle had the key he'd been given on that first day when he went to pick up the computer. They let themselves inside and then looked around the empty house. It was so odd to be in Nolan's home when the man wasn't there. It didn't appear that anything had been disturbed since the day Nolan had been found dead.

"Any idea where to start?" Kyle asked.

"I guess his office in the back, or maybe his bedroom. Hazel said he was making notes in a small notebook. Maybe it's still in his jacket pocket."

Kyle and Tj began to methodically look through Nolan's things. It felt like an invasion of his privacy, but Tj wasn't certain what else to do. If Nolan had a lead they'd yet to discover they needed to find it. Otherwise Tj would be forced to tell Roy what she suspected of Brandon.

Tj continued to search the house while Kyle headed back to the shed Nolan had used as an office. The odds were that the killer had known about the notebook, found it, and took it with him on the day of the murder. Tj remembered Nolan joking about hiding things in plain sight. The obvious place to hide a book was on a bookshelf, so Tj began searching through the shelves in his spare room. When she came across the notebook even she was surprised it was that easy.

She was sitting on the floor so she leaned back on her heels and began to read. "Oh my God!" Tj heard the back door open, followed by footsteps. "You'll never guess what I found," Tj yelled.

She stood up and started toward the door only to find Kyle standing in the hall with a gun at his back.

"You killed Nolan," Tj said to the man standing behind Kyle.

"I had to."

"What do you mean, you had to?"

"He found out about everything. I was going to go to jail for a long time. Do you have any idea what happens to cops in jail?"

Tj frowned, and then suddenly everything made sense. "Brandon didn't kill Clay Warner; you did."

"The man deserved to die. It almost killed Andrea when they set him free. In retrospect, killing the man might not have been the best move, but I was in love with her, and I think she cared about me. We had a future together, and then Clay Warner came along and ruined everything."

"Wait—I get why you killed Warner, but how does his death fit in with the rest?"

"What rest?"

"The missing files at the shooting range," Tj said. "You must have taken them."

"They had my signature all over them," Tim Matthews admitted. "I was afraid that seeing my signature might cause you or Roy to become suspicious."

"You stole the gun you used to kill Clay Warner," Tj realized.

"Everyone knew I planned to attend the police academy after I graduated high school. I used to go to the range to shoot all the time. When I saw how insane poor Andrea was, I checked out a gun and snuck out with it hidden under my coat. The guy who worked at the armory was clueless; guns walked away all the time."

"So you realized that if someone looked at the log they would see that you checked out a gun on the day Clay Warner died. Why take eight months' worth of files?"

"It would seem more suspect to only take the file I needed."

"Smart. And the phone call to Murphy's Bar?"

"A decoy. I made the call and then put the phone back in Nolan's pocket. I figured you'd find the phone and fixate on the call. It worked for a while. Should have known you'd be smart enough not to waste too much time working on a dead end."

Tj looked at Tim. "Are you going to kill me?"

Tim started to cry. "I don't want to."

Tj looked Tim directly in the eye. "I asked you if you were going to kill me."

Tim's hand began to shake. He seemed focused exclusively on Tj and didn't notice Kyle step to the side.

"If you're going to kill me, I need you to look me in the eye while you do it," Tj insisted.

Tim was crying so hard that Tj knew he couldn't see what he was doing. She nodded to Kyle, who said something to get Tim's attention. When Tim turned his head Tj knocked the gun from his hand. Damn. That move was proving to be handy in all these murder cases.

CHAPTER 16

"I can't believe Tim Matthews killed Nolan." Ben shook his head in sorrow later that evening. "Tim is such a good guy, and a good cop. It makes no sense."

"I guess he felt like his back was against the wall," Mike said sympathetically.

"Yeah, but Nolan?" Doc looked pale and defeated.

"Do you think Nolan would have turned Tim in for what he did fifteen years ago?" Tj asked.

"I don't know," Ben admitted. "He killed a man. A scumbag of a man, but still a man."

"Tim is right," Doc commented. "He won't last a week in prison. Cops never do well when they become prisoners."

"I'm sure they'll make special arrangements," Tj speculated.

"Won't help," Doc predicted.

"Roy must be devastated," Mike added. "The two of them were so close."

"I don't see how he's going to go on," Tj agreed.

"Is Kyle with Andrea?" Doc asked.

"He took her to the airport. I think she decided to get out of town before someone told her she couldn't leave. Of course, I don't know who would tell her to stick around because I don't think there's a deputy on staff in Serenity this evening. Roy is with Tim and has asked for immediate leave. I imagine they're sending someone up from Indulgence to cover until Roy gets back. Kyle said he'd come by when he got back into town."

"And Hunter?" Ben asked.

"He's picking up his grandfather and heading over. He said Jake would want to be here with all of you this evening," Tj answered. "Jenna's on her way over with Dennis and Helen's coming to pick up the girls. She's planning to let all four girls spend the night at her place, and she's dropping Stella at a friend's. I've called over to the Grill and they're going to drop off some food, so we can all settle in and take the time we need to process what's happened."

"When Nolan died I really thought that would be the darkest day of the year, but this..." Ben left the sentence unfinished.

"I can't imagine what was going through Nolan's mind when he realized why Tim was there," Mike commented. "The two men had been friends and colleagues."

Tj almost felt like Tim had died. She supposed in a way he had. The Tim she knew and loved had been replaced by a man who would kill an unarmed friend. It was going to take the town and its residents quite a while to recover from the shock.

CHAPTER 17

Tuesday, March 24

"Do you see that little girl over there?" Tj whispered to Kyle. They were in Grainger's General Store buying yet another replacement jacket for Gracie, the third she'd bought her since school had started in September. "I think she's wearing Gracie's jacket."

"That's Sally Bentifield," Kyle commented. "She's in Gracie's class."

"How do you know that?" Tj asked.

"Her sister Siobhan is in your choir. Sometimes Sally comes to rehearsal with her. It seems their mom is working two jobs to try to make ends meet and the dad isn't in the picture. Siobhan has to babysit her younger siblings, so I told her it was okay for them to come to watch."

"Do you think she stole Gracie's coat?" Tj asked.

Kyle scrunched up his face. "Of course she didn't steal Gracie's coat. She's a good kid. She probably has a coat like the one Gracie lost. You did buy it here, after all. I'm sure there are a lot of first graders in town with the same coat."

Tj glared at the dark-haired little girl, but Kyle was right. There were probably a dozen kids in town with the same coat. Tj returned to her task of selecting Gracie's next coat as Sally's sister walked over to where the girl was waiting in line to pay for whatever it was she was clutching to her chest.

Tj gasped. "Now I know something is going on. It looks like the sister has a coat just like the one Gracie lost a few months ago. What are the odds that the two sisters would both have coats that look exactly like the ones that used to belong to Gracie? I'm going to talk to them."

"Tj, wait," Kyle called, but she wasn't listening.

"Hi," Tj began. "I'm Tj Jensen. I'm Gracie's sister. I believe Gracie is in your class?"

"Yes," Sally said.

"Well, she lost a coat that looks just like the one you're wearing, and I was wondering if perhaps you found it."

The little girl's eyes filled with tears. She looked scared to death. "I didn't find it," the girl cried. "Gracie gave it to me. She gave one to Sarah too." She nodded toward her twin sister.

"She *gave* you the coats?"

"She said they were old and she had a new one. She gave us the matching gloves and hats too. I hope it was okay. We didn't mean to do anything wrong." The girl set the loaf of bread she was holding on the ground and began to take off her jacket. The shirt she had on beneath it was threadbare. "You can have it back if you want." The girl held the coat out in front of her.

Suddenly Tj felt like the biggest heel ever to walk the face of the earth.

"No, sweetie. You can keep the coat. Sarah too. I think I

might have gotten confused. I guess this is Gracie's old coat. Silly me; I thought it was her new coat. I'm sorry if I scared you. Here, let me pay for your bread."

"No, ma'am. Mama says we don't take no charity. We can pay for our bread. It's a day old, so Mrs. Grainger always gives it to us for a dime."

A dime?

"Okay, well, I'm sorry I got confused. Enjoy the rest of your day." Tj skulked back to Kyle. She couldn't remember the last time she'd felt so bad. "Sally said Gracie gave her the jacket. Gracie told her it was her old one and she had a new one, so she didn't need it. Do you think Gracie was trying to get a new coat?"

"Or maybe she was helping out a friend in need? From what I know about the family, they're pretty poor, but the mom won't accept any help from anyone who wants to help her," Kyle informed her.

"But Gracie has lost three coats this year. Do you think she gave them all away?"

"If I know Gracie, that's exactly what she did."

Tj realized that Kyle was right. Gracie had a tender heart. If she saw that one of her classmates needed a coat or gloves she wouldn't think twice about giving them hers.

"I feel like an idiot." Tj sighed. "I wonder why Gracie didn't tell me what she was doing."

"Maybe she thought you'd be mad."

"Yeah. And rightfully so. I've been reading her the riot act about losing her things. I even made her go to bed without television the other night and she never said a word about why her coats kept turning up missing. I guess I'd better talk to her."

"Yeah," Kyle agreed. "That might be a good idea."

Tj placed two coats and two matching hat, glove, and scarf sets in her basket. One for Gracie to wear and one for her to give away.

"You know, you've got one great kid." Kyle put his arm around Tj.

"Yeah. I really do."

For the first time since Nolan was murdered by a man he trusted implicitly, Tj felt a ray of hope that, just perhaps, the world was a place where love and selflessness could prevail over hatred and fear.

"Do you want to get a drink after we are done here?" Kyle asked.

"I'd love to but only a fast drink. I have a date with Hunter tonight. A real date which I am determined not to mess up with my doubts and insecurities."

A strange look crossed Kyles face.

"Is anything wrong?" Tj asked.

Kyle smiled. "No. Nothing's wrong. I'm glad that you have decided to work on your relationship with Hunter. He's a good guy."

"Yeah he really is. I know he hurt me in the past but he's changed. We both have. I really think we can make it this time."

"Relationships take work but from what I've observed they are worth the effort."

"It's so odd but I'm really nervous. I know that is weird. I've known Hunter for the majority of my life and I am usually totally comfortable with him but as crazy as it sounds I'm a bundle of nerves now that I've finally committed to taking things to the next level in our relationship."

"It's a big step and you've been stressing over it for quite some time. I think it is totally normal to be nervous. I'm sure that once you get those first awkward minutes out of the way you'll settle back into the comfort zone the two of you have always shared."

"You think so? I keep thinking the nerves are an indication that I'm making the wrong choice."

"Do you think you're making the wrong choice?"

"No. Of course not. There is really no reason for Hunter and me not to be together. I love him and he loves me and our relationship will thrill both of our grandfathers. Let's pay for this stuff and get that drink. I can really use one to settle my nerves."

Kyle and headed to the counter where Tj paid for Gracie's jacket and then the pair headed down the street to the bar. They found a table in the corner near the back and each ordered a beer.

"So did you ever find out which deputy made the mistake that set Clay free and who set the second fire?" Kyle asked.

"No. Roy and I both suspect it was Boggs who both made the mistake and set the second fire but we can't prove it. The level of cooperation we've had trying to get information from the county has been so incredibly nonexistent that the only thing that makes sense is that Boggs is covering his own butt. I spoke briefly to Roy about it and it is his opinion that if the guilty party was any of the other three Boggs wouldn't think twice about making the information public especially with the upheaval in the sheriff's department due to Tim's arrest. The problem is that Boggs is in a position to destroy whatever documents need to be destroyed so there may never be a way to uncover the truth."

"And the others aren't talking?"

Tj shook her head. "Jerry Johnson still works for Boggs and seems unwilling to talk about the situation at all. I guess I don't blame him. He is close to retirement and Boggs has the power to make his last years miserable if he gets it in his head to do so. Max Stevens confided to grandpa that the evidence found in Clay's house which led to his arrest looked suspicious. He told grandpa that he wouldn't be at all surprised to find that the gasoline, fuses, and glass bottles had been planted. Max swears he didn't do plant the evidence or set the second fire and he really doesn't know for certain who did but his money is on Boggs as the bad guy as well."

"And Dover Wood?"

"He seemed to be cooperating at first but he has clammed up as well. I'm going to bet that Boggs got to him. I'm not sure we'll ever know for sure what occurred that ended up allowing Clay to go free."

"It really is a tragedy," Kyle shook his head. "Some cop decides to take a short cut and take the law into his own hands by setting up the person they suspected of setting the fire and then a basically good guy like Tim gets caught up in the aftermath totally destroying his life."

"The entire situation makes me nuts but I know that my anger won't free Tim or bring Nolan back. Grandpa talked to Judge Harper who seemed to think that Boggs is going to retire at the end of this term. If he has done everything we suspect him of doing he deserves to rot in jail. It is totally unfair that he is getting off scot-free, but I guess sometimes life isn't fair."

Kyle took a sip of his beer. "Maybe Jerry or Dover will grow a conscious and tell what they know."

"We can only hope that justice will prevail and in the end the good guys will win and the bad guys will get what they deserve. By the way, I'm sorry Andrea left. It seemed like the two of you really hit it off."

Kyle shrugged. "Andrea was great and we had a lot of fun but she's not the one I'm waiting for."

"The one? Is there a one?"

"A metaphorical *one* that is always mentioned in romance novels when the hero or heroine realizes that he or she has found the *one* they've been waiting for."

"Kyle Donovan do you read romance novels?'

Kyle blushed.

"You do read romance novels."

"Hey most are well written and entertaining."

Tj leaned over and kissed Kyle on the cheek. "That's what I love about you. You are so diverse." Tj glanced at her watch. "Oh I gotta run. I told Hunter I'd be at his house by seven but before I do I wanted to ask about the choir. The kids were asking if you are going to help out next year."

"If by help out you mean run the program while you watch from the sidelines and take all the credit I'd love to," Kyle teased.

"I don't take all the credit."

Kyle tilted his head to the side as if to offer a counter point.

"Okay maybe I do take all the credit with Principal Remington but while I might get the credit you get all the love. The kids love you, the parents love you, I love you. Isn't that enough?"

Kyle smiled. "More than enough. You'd better hurry. You don't want to keep Hunter waiting."

"Yeah I should go." Tj hugged Kyle. "Thanks for everything you do for me. I'll see you tomorrow."

Tj turned as she was about to exit the bar. She couldn't help but notice that Kyle looked sad. Maybe he was missing Andrea more than he let on. She really did hope that Kyle found the one that his heart longed for. There wasn't anyone on this earth that deserved happiness more than he did.

KATHI DALEY

Kathi Daley lives with her husband, kids, grandkids, and Bernese mountain dogs in beautiful Lake Tahoe. When she isn't writing, she likes to read (preferably at the beach or by the fire), cook (preferably something with chocolate or cheese), and garden (planting and planning, not weeding). She also enjoys spending time in the water, hiking, biking, and snowshoeing. Kathi uses the mountain setting in which she lives, along with the animals (wild and domestic) that share her home, as inspiration for her five cozy mystery series: Zoe Donovan, Whales and Tails Island, Tj Jensen, Sand and Sea Hawaiian, and Seacliff High Teen.

**The Tj Jensen Mystery Series
by Kathi Daley**

Henery Press Mystery Books

And finally, before you go...
Here are a few other mysteries
you might enjoy:

TELL ME NO LIES

Lynn Chandler Willis

An Ava Logan Mystery (#1)

Ava Logan, single mother and small business owner, lives deep in the heart of the Appalachian Mountains, where poverty and pride reign. As publisher of the town newspaper, she's busy balancing election season stories and a rash of ginseng thieves.

And then the story gets personal. After her friend is murdered, Ava digs for the truth all the while juggling her two teenage children, her friend's orphaned toddler, and her own muddied past. Faced with threats against those closest to her, Ava must find the killer before she, or someone she loves, ends up dead.

Available at booksellers nationwide and online

Visit www.henerypress.com for details

MURDER ON A SILVER PLATTER

Shawn Reilly Simmons

A Red Carpet Catering Mystery (#1)

Penelope Sutherland and her Red Carpet Catering company just got their big break as the on-set caterer for an upcoming blockbuster. But when she discovers a dead body outside her house, Penelope finds herself in hot water. Things start to boil over when serious accidents threaten the lives of the cast and crew. And when the film's star, who happens to be Penelope's best friend, is poisoned, the entire production is nearly shut down.

Threats and accusations send Penelope out of the frying pan and into the fire as she struggles to keep her company afloat. Before Penelope can dish up dessert, she must find the killer or she'll be the one served up on a silver platter.

Available at booksellers nationwide and online

Visit www.henerypress.com for details

PRACTICAL SINS
FOR COLD CLIMATES
Shelley Costa

A Val Cameron Mystery (#1)

When Val Cameron, a Senior Editor with a New York publishing company, is sent to the Canadian Northwoods to sign a reclusive bestselling author to a contract, she soon discovers she is definitely out of her element. Val is convinced she can persuade the author of that blockbuster, The Nebula Covenant, to sign with her, but first she has to find him.

Aided by a float plane pilot whose wife was murdered two years ago in a case gone cold, Val's hunt for the recluse takes on new meaning: can she clear him of suspicion in that murder before she links her own professional fortunes to the publication of his new book?

When she finds herself thrown into a wilderness lake community where livelihoods collide, Val wonders whether the prospect of running into a bear might be the least of her problems.

Available at booksellers nationwide and online

Visit www.henerypress.com for details

CPSIA information can be obtained
at www.ICGtesting.com
Printed in the USA
LVHW051109240623
750702LV00010B/806